CHRISTMAS AT
THE TYCOON'S
COMMAND

CHRISTMAS AT THE TYCOON'S COMMAND

JENNIFER HAYWARD

MILLS & BOON

First published in Great Britain 2017
by Mills & Boon, an imprint of HarperCollins*Publishers*
1 London Bridge Street, London, SE1 9GF

Large Print edition 2018

© 2017 Jennifer Drogell

ISBN: 978-0-263-07359-1

MIX
Paper from
responsible sources
FSC® C007454

This book is produced from independently certified
FSC™ paper to ensure responsible forest management.
For more information visit www.harpercollins.co.uk/green.

Printed and bound in Great Britain
by CPI Group (UK) Ltd, Croydon, CR0 4YY

For my editor, Nic.

I couldn't have written this without
your guidance and inspiration.

You are amazing and I look forward to
working on many great books together.

CHAPTER ONE

SHE WAS NOT losing this one.

Chloe Russo fixed her gaze on the bright yellow taxi that had appeared like an apparition from heaven in the ferociously snarled First Avenue traffic, its lit number her only chance at salvation in the monsoon that had descended over Manhattan.

Shielding her eyes from the driving rain, she stepped a foot deeper into the layers of honking, snarling traffic and jammed her hand high in the air. The driver of a Bentley sounded his horn furiously as he swerved to avoid her, but Chloe, heart pounding, kept her eyes glued to the taxi driver's face, willing him to stop.

The taxi slid to a halt in front of her in a cacophony of screeching horns and spraying water. Heart soaring, she waded through the giant puddle that stood between her and victory, flung the door of the taxi open and slid inside, reeling off

Evolution's Fifth Avenue address with a request to step on it that made the cabbie roll his eyes.

"Lady," he muttered caustically, "have you *looked* outside?"

She'd been *standing* in it for half an hour, she wanted to scream. While thirty-five of his co-workers had passed her by—she knew because she'd counted every one of them. But picking a fight with the last remaining cab driver in Manhattan seemed unwise, given her present situation.

She was late for her first board meeting as the director of Evolution's fragrance division. An inauspicious start.

Her teeth chattered amid a chill that seemed to reach bone-deep. She pushed off the hood of her raincoat and mopped her face with a tissue, thankful for her waterproof mascara. Let out a defeated sigh. She should have left earlier. Had forgotten taxis on a rainy day in Manhattan were akin to spotting a western lowland gorilla in the wild. But in truth, she'd been dreading today and everything about it.

Her cell phone vibrated in her bag. She rooted around to find it as a loud pop song joined the symphony of honking horns. Fingers curling around the sleek metal, she pulled it out and answered it before her grumpy driver deposited her back into the downpour.

"I just landed," her sister, Mireille, announced. "How are you? How was your flight? Did you get settled in okay? It's *so* amazing to have you back in New York."

The verbal torrent pulled a smile from her lips. "Good, good and yes. Although it just took me half an hour to get a taxi. I'm soaked to the bone."

"You've been living in Europe too long." Her sister's voice lowered to a conspiratorial whisper. "Of course, I'm really calling to see how your dinner with Nico went. I've been dying to know. Uncle Giorgio has himself all in a dither with this campaign of his to unseat him."

Chloe bit her lip. Nico Di Fiore, the new CEO of Evolution, her family cosmetic company, was a loaded subject of late. Her late father's godson, Nico had been appointed CEO upon her parents' deaths last spring according to the terms of her father's will, assuming a position that should have been her uncle Giorgio's. He had also been appointed financial regent for Chloe and Mireille until they reached the age of thirty, an unexpected and unacceptable development that had been the last straw for Chloe, because it meant four years of *him* in her life.

"I didn't have dinner with him." Her offhand tone hid the apprehension dampening her palms. "I wanted to keep things professional. I suggested we meet tomorrow instead—on my first day back."

Mireille drew in a breath. "You *blew* Nico off for dinner?"

"It wasn't like that." Except it had been exactly like that.

There was a pregnant pause on the other end of the line. "That really wasn't wise, Chloe."

"He *summoned* me to have dinner with him," she came back defensively. Just like he'd *summoned* her home from Paris, where she'd been perfectly happy. "This is *our* company, not his. Isn't it driving you crazy having him in charge?"

"It was what Father wanted." Mireille sighed. "I know Evolution's your baby—far more than it is mine. That Uncle Giorgio has you all wound up, but you need to face reality. Nico is leading the company. I don't know what's going on between you two, but you're going to have to come to terms with it."

"There's nothing going on between us." Hadn't been since Nico had broken her heart far too many years ago to remember now. And she *had* been attempting to do exactly that—to process this new reality that had seen Nico take over Evolution when her parents had been killed in a car crash in Tuscany six months ago, turning her life upside down in the process. But she couldn't quite seem to get there.

Evolution's stately, soaring, gold-tinted headquarters rose majestically in front of her as the taxi turned onto Fifth Avenue. A fist formed in her chest, making it hard to breathe.

"I have to go," she murmured. "It's the board meeting tonight."

"Right." A wealth of meaning in her sister's tone. "Better you than me." As a junior executive in Evolution's PR department, Chloe's younger sister was not a member of the board. "Promise me you won't fight with him, Chloe."

"That," she said grimly, "is impossible. I love you and I'll see you tomorrow."

She handed the taxi driver the fare as he pulled

to a halt in front of the building. Slid out of the car and stepped onto the sidewalk, teeming with its usual wall-to-wall pedestrian traffic huddled under brightly colored umbrellas.

A frozen feeling descended over her as she stood staring up at the giant gold letters that spelled out *Evolution* on the front of the building. Her parents—Martino and Juliette Russo— had spent two decades building Evolution into a legendary cosmetics brand. They had been the heart and soul of the company. *Of her.*

She hadn't been in the building since she'd lost them, buried in work in the Paris lab. The thought of going in there now without them present seemed like the final admission they were gone, and she couldn't quite seem to do it.

The crowd parted like a river around her as she stood there, heart in her mouth, feet glued to the concrete. A woman in a Gucci raincoat finally jolted her out of her suspended state, crankily advising her to "move on." Her fingers clutched tight around her bag, she made her way through the glass doors, presented the security guard with her credentials and rode the elevator to the fiftieth floor, where Evolution's executive offices overlooked Central Park.

A slim, blond-haired woman with trendy glasses pounced on her as she emerged into the elegant cream marble reception area. "Clara Jones, your new PA," the blonde introduced herself, relieving Chloe of her dripping raincoat in the same breath. "You're the last to arrive. Nico is—well, you know…" she said, giving Chloe a meaningful look. "He likes to start on time."

Her heart crawled into her throat. "I couldn't get a cab."

"It *is* awful out there."

Clara led Chloe down the hall toward the large, plush conference room with its expansive view of a wintry, lamp-lit Central Park. "Nico gave me your presentation. It's ready to go."

Now if only she was. Memories deluged her as she stood surveying the crowded, warmly lit room full of Evolution board members and directors enjoying a glass of wine and hors d'oeuvres before the meeting began. Of her father manning the seat at the head of the table that Nico now would as the chairman of the board. Of her mother swanning around, captivating the executives with her sparkling wit and charm.

Her stomach swam with nerves. She was a *scientist*. Her mother had been a self-made genius with a larger-than-life personality who'd created a multibillion-dollar empire out of a tiny bath products company she'd founded to serve her husband's financial clientele. Chloe was far more comfortable in the lab creating beautiful things than presenting to a stiff-suited board like her mother had been. But this was her job now. A necessary evil.

Any nerves about her presentation, however, faded to the background as Nico spotted her. Clad in a sleek, dark gray Tom Ford suit, the white shirt and silver tie he wore beneath it making the most of his dark good looks and olive skin, he was faultlessly elegant. It was when she lifted her gaze to his that she realized just how much trouble she was in.

His lips set in a flat line, jaw locked, smoky gray gaze full of thunderclouds, he was *furious*. Fingers of ice crept up her spine as he murmured something to the board member he was speaking with, then set his tall, impressive frame into motion, eating up the distance between them. Clara took one look at his face, muttered something about checking the AV equipment and disappeared.

Chloe's heart ricocheted in a hard drumbeat against her ribs as Nico came to a halt in front of her. She tipped her head back to look up at him, refusing to reveal how much he intimidated her. With his leonine dark head, cold, slate blue eyes and cheekbones at forty-five degrees, he couldn't quite be called handsome in the traditional sense because he was far too hard for that.

His wide, full mouth made up for that lack of softness, however—lush and almost pouty when he wanted to seduce a response out of the person in question. Which was not now.

Her heart battered up against her chest in another wave of nerves at the dark fire in his eyes. At the realization that any hope she'd had that she'd developed an immunity to him after seven years in Europe had been utter self-delusion. That the man she'd once thought had been *the one* had hardened into a ruthless, sapphire-edged version of himself she couldn't hope to know.

She might hate him, she *did* hate him for teaching her the cruel lesson he had, but he was still the most potently gorgeous male she'd ever encountered.

"I'm sorry," she murmured, forcing the words past a constricted throat. "I forgot it's impossible to get a cab in Manhattan on a rainy day."

His stormy gaze darkened. "We'll discuss it afterward," he said quietly, so quietly it sent her pulse skittering into a dead run. "Take ten minutes to say hello and we'll start."

She nodded. Forced herself through the round of small talk, latching gratefully on to her uncle Giorgio, Evolution's flamboyant director of marketing, before Nico called the meeting to order.

An undeniably compelling speaker, he outlined the big picture as Evolution headed into its first Christmas season without its cofounders. Investor confidence was shaky, he observed candidly—the company's stock price in trouble—with the world worried the loss of Juliette Russo, the creative force of the company, would strike a death knell for Evolution.

Chloe's heart sank as he went on to detail the keys for a successful path forward. It wasn't true that Evolution was a fading star. Her parents had built a company rich with talent. Vivre, the line of fragrances Chloe had spent three years developing with one of the most brilliant French perfumers, *would* be the hit Christmas product the company needed. But, she reminded herself, the world didn't know that yet.

Nico called her up last in the parade of directors presenting their holiday season highlights, after the head of the skincare division had made a big splash with his luxurious, all-natural skincare line. She suspected Nico did it on purpose.

She rose on legs the consistency of jelly, smoothed the pencil skirt of her still-damp suit and moved to the front of the room. Hands clammy, mouth full of sawdust, she clicked the remote to begin the presentation. Focusing on her passion for her work, she began. Too fast and clunky in her delivery at first, she gradually relaxed as she explained her vision for Vivre and the aspirational campaign that would accompany it. It will, she told those assembled, redefine how beauty is framed in a world that badly needs inspiration.

Instead of salivating over her exciting launch plan that featured celebrities who would spread the inspirational message, the board members peppered her with questions.

"Isn't the perfume market oversaturated?"

"Your mother could have sold this, but can you?"

"What about all the workplaces that are going scent-free?"

"Wouldn't it be better to focus on the all-natural products that are dominating the market?"

She took a deep breath and answered the questions the best she could. She had been working with her mother in the lab ever since she was a little girl, she told them. She knew where the magic was. She already had her own signature fragrances to back her up. And the celebrity endorsement she had planned for the Vivre campaign would help her create the buzz she needed.

When she ran out of answers and needed big-picture help, she looked to Nico because she didn't have that backup in her head. But instead of coming to her rescue, he sat back in his chair, arms crossed over his chest, and focused that glittering gray gaze of his on her.

Her stomach swooped. He was punishing her.

The bastard. She looked at the director of the skincare division, who stared blankly back at her, clearly not about to help either and diminish his own product line. A trickle of perspiration ran down her back.

Finally, her uncle stepped in with a passionate rebuttal, reminding the board of the founding tenants Evolution was built on—luxury perfumes like Vivre that had taken the world by storm. But by then, her credibility was in tatters.

Answering the final question, she sat down red-faced.

Nico held on to his temper by the threads it had been hanging from all evening as the last board member disappeared toward the elevators and home.

"My office," he murmured in Chloe's ear. *"Now."*

Head tossed back, she stalked out of the room in front of him and down the hall toward his office. It would be difficult, he surmised, eyeing her curvaceous backside, for her to find it when she had no idea where it was.

She came to a sliding halt in front of the sophisticated lounge that was a new addition to the executive floor, her gaze moving over the photos of the company's cofounders gracing the walls.

"What happened to my father's office?" she demanded, spinning on her heel, dark eyes flashing. "Or couldn't you even leave that alone?"

"I didn't think it was appropriate for me to assume it," he murmured, directing her down the hall toward his office with a hand at her back. Something in him hadn't been able to simply wipe his mentor from existence by redecorating a space that had always been quintessentially Martino's. But he didn't feel the need to explain his actions to Chloe at this particular moment. He was barely resisting the urge to strangle her for the ever-present recalcitrance that had pushed him one step too far this time.

He closed the door to his office with a decisive click. Strode to the window and counted to ten because that was what Chloe did to him. Pushed buttons he didn't even know he had. Elicited emotions he had always had to exert the most extreme self-control to silence. Because Chloe was the chink in his armor. The one weakness he couldn't seem to kick. And wanting her had always been a swift trip to hell.

"You were punishing me, weren't you?" Her voice drifted over his shoulder, trembling with rage.

He turned around and leaned against the sill. Studied the fury on her beautiful face. The way her delicate features had settled into an intriguing beauty that was impossible to ignore. The arms she had crossed over her firm, high breasts, the feet defiantly planted apart in her haute couture Parisian suit.

She was a study in rebellion. It was insane the fire that rose up inside him, the desire to crush those lush lips into submission under his own, to shock her out of the self-protective state she'd descended into since her parents' passing. To unearth *some* sign the passionate Chloe he knew still existed.

But having her had never been an option for him. He had conditioned it out of himself a long time ago because he'd had to. Just like he'd eliminated every other undesirable need he'd had in a life that had never had any room for self-indulgence.

He pointed at the chair in front of his desk. "Sit."

She crossed her arms tighter over her chest. "I'd prefer to stand."

"Bene." He took a seat on the corner of his desk, eyes on her. "I hung you out to dry in there because you needed to learn a lesson."

"That you are the king of the castle," she challenged, eyes flashing.

"Yes," he said evenly. "I am. And the sooner you realize it, the easier this is going to be on both of us. It was your father's wish, Chloe, that I run this company. And while I don't intend for one minute to deny you your place at the center of it—in fact, my intention is the opposite—you need to get that particular fact straight in your head."

Her mouth curled. "Giorgio should be the head of this company, not you."

"That's why your father made me second in command a year ago?" he rebutted coolly. "Think rationally."

She flicked a wrist at him, ebony eyes snapping with heat. "Because you somehow *brainwashed* him into it. How else would his will have been so *perfectly* in order when he died? Because it was your master plan, of course."

A low curl of heat unfurled inside him. "Watch it," he said softly. "You're starting to sound like your very bitter, very deluded uncle. Martino put me in control of Evolution in the event something happened to him and Juliette because he knew Giorgio would drive the company into the ground with his big spending ways. Your uncle has neither the business brain nor the common sense to run Evolution."

"That's a lie," she breathed. "He is widely reputed to be one of the most brilliant marketers there is. And don't forget," she added, eyes darkening with old wounds, "I have firsthand knowledge of how ambitious you are, Nico. Success is the only thing that matters to you."

"And *that*," he said, emphasizing the word, "is the problem between us, Chloe. I am grieving, too. We are *all* grieving. And yet you are fixated on ancient history when it has no place here. You need to grow up and move on."

Her eyes widened. "I am *not* bringing the personal into this."

"Aren't you?" He slid his gaze over her fire-soaked cheeks. "That's why you've spent the last six months hiding away in Paris instead of taking your place in this company? So I finally had to *order* you back? Because there's nothing personal here?"

A muscle pulled tight at the corner of her mouth. "You have *such* an overinflated ego. Vivre wasn't ready."

"So you said," he responded quietly. "My contacts in the lab say it was ready six months ago. That you have been stalling, perfecting imperfections that don't exist." He fixed his gaze on hers. "Hide from the world or hide from me, Chloe, both of them are ending now."

She glared at him. "I *hate you*."

"I know." He'd decided a long time ago that was preferable in this relationship of theirs.

She drew a visible breath that rippled through her slim body as she collected her composure. "Have you reviewed my launch plan, then? Since Vivre is so clearly *ready*?"

"Yes," he murmured, picking it up off his desk. "*This* is what I think of it."

Her eyes went as big as saucers as he tossed the sheaf of papers into the wastebasket. "What *are* you doing?"

"Putting it where it belongs." He shook his

head, his hands coming to rest on the edge of the desk. "You have no business case in that plan. All you have is fluffy, overinflated, feel-good market research that relies on your legacy to sell it. A *fifty-million-dollar* launch plan in which the linchpin for success turns on a celebrity endorsement program you don't have a hope in hell of attaining."

Her chin lifted. "That is a *brilliant* launch plan, Nico. I have a *master's* degree, in case you had forgotten. Maybe I should have been more detailed with the numbers—and I *can* be because I was focusing on the big picture—but the consumer testing has been off the charts for Vivre. One of the most important French perfumers in the industry thinks it's inspired—as brilliant as anything my mother has done. *This* is the product that is going to prove Evolution is back this Christmas, not some generic all-natural skincare line you couldn't distinguish from any of its competitors."

He surveyed her flushed, determined face. The passion that had been missing for months. "I am backing Emilio's skincare line for the holiday push. I agree with the board."

Her jaw slackened. "That's *insane*. This company was built on our signature perfumes. People are looking for an inspirational campaign from us. That's what we do—*we inspire*."

"And you," he pointed out, "delivered the product late. Even if I did approve the campaign, it's the beginning of October. You'd never get it into market in time."

She faltered for the first time. Because he was right and she knew it. He was not, however, oblivious to the fact that Chloe was a genius. That she had her mother's touch. That the success of Evolution rested on her shoulders as Juliette, her mother, had known it would. But sinking fifty million dollars into an impossible-to-execute holiday campaign would be foolhardy when the company desperately needed a Christmas hit.

"Work with the sales and marketing team," he said. "Show me the numbers. Lay the timeline out for me so I know it can work. And," he qualified, "and this is a big *but*, the only way I'd ever green-light a launch plan like this is if you can supply the big-name celebrities you've earmarked up front. Which is very unlikely given the hit the brand has taken. So, consider a plan B."

"There is no plan B," she said flatly. "I chose those celebrities because of their personal history. Because they embody the spirit of the perfumes. I created them with them in mind. If I can talk to them, if they can experience the fragrances, *understand* the message I'm trying to tell, I know I can convince them to do it."

He absorbed the energy that surrounded her. The unshakable belief in what she had created. And wondered if she realized the campaign was about *her*. About the battle she had always fought within herself to shine in the shadow of her charismatic mother and stunning sister.

"Prove me wrong, then," he challenged. "Give me what I'm asking for. But know this, Chloe. Your flashy degree is worth nothing in the real world until you prove you know how to use it. *I* can help you do that. Your father *asked* me to provide that mentorship to you. But I have better things to do than babysit you if you're not willing to learn."

"Babysit?" The word dripped with scorn.

"You're not satisfied with ruling me financially? Now you need to master me professionally?"

His mouth tightened. "That is exactly the kind of attitude I'm talking about. Every time I try to forge a working relationship between us, you shut me down. You're mysteriously lost in the lab. You're too busy to talk. That ends now."

"I don't do that," she rejected. "I've been extremely busy."

"Unfortunate for you tonight." He rubbed a palm over his jaw. "Here's how it's going to work from here on out. I'll give you the rest of the week to get settled in. To iron out your launch plan. You come back to me with the details and we decide how to move forward.

"Second, we'll start having regular morning meetings beginning next week. I can teach you the business end of things and we can check in with each other as needed. That's what your father did with me. And," he added, pausing for emphasis, "you *will* attempt to listen rather than fight with me at every turn."

A stony look back.

"Finally," he concluded, "we will begin building your profile with the press. The PR department is going to schedule a training session for you."

Her chin dipped. "I'm terrible with the media. I either clam up or say things I shouldn't. Let Giorgio do it."

"Giorgio is not the future of this company. *You* are. You'll learn to do better."

Resistance wrote itself in every line of her delicate body, her dark eyes shimmering with fire. "Are you done, then? With all your ground rules? Because I'm exhausted and I'd like to go home. The time difference is catching up with me."

"One more," he said softly, eyes on hers. "I am your boss, Chloe. Hate me all you want in private, but in public you *will* show me the respect I'm due."

CHAPTER TWO

CHLOE WAS STILL fuming over her encounter with Nico the next morning as she woke up to brilliant sunshine in her cozy townhouse on the Upper East Side. It was almost as if last night's monsoon had never happened. Everything looking sparkly and brand-new on a crisp fall day that was perfection in Manhattan.

A grimace twisted her mouth. Now if only she could say the same for her combative showdown with Nico.

She slid out of bed, threw on a robe and made herself some coffee in an attempt to regain her equilibrium. Java in hand, she wandered to the French doors that looked out over the street and drank in the sleepy little neighborhood she now called home.

A splendor of gold and rust, the vivid splash of color from the changing leaves of the stately old trees was the perfect contrast to the cream stuccoed townhouses that lined the street. She and Mireille had fallen in love with the neighborhood one Sunday afternoon on a walk through the village. Her father had bought them each a townhouse side by side, Chloe's in anticipation of her return home to New York to take her place at Evolution, Mireille, while she studied public relations at school.

We know you're too independent to come home and live with us, her father had teased. *But we want you close.*

A wave of bitter loneliness settled over her. She wrapped her arms around herself, coffee cup cradled against her chest. Usually she managed to keep the hollow emptiness at bay—burying herself in her lab until she crawled into bed at night. But this morning it seemed to throb from the inside out, scraping her raw.

She missed her parents. So desperately much she had no idea how to even verbalize it. How to release the emotion that had been stuck inside her so long lest it swamp her so completely when she did, she would never emerge whole. Because her parents had been her glue, her innocence, the force that had shielded her from the world. And now that they were gone, she didn't know how to restore the status quo. Didn't know how to reset herself. Didn't know how to *feel* anymore.

She was *scared* to feel.

Her mother had been her best friend. A bright, vivid star that bathed you in its warmth—their shared passion bonding them from their earliest days. Her father, the wisest, smartest man she'd ever known, with a heart so big it had seemed limitless. He would be furious if he saw her like this, because Nico was right—she had been hiding, from the world and from herself.

She hugged her arms tighter around her chest as she watched the neighborhood stir to life. She needed to move on. Nico had also been right in that. Paris was no longer her life. New York was now. Assuming the role her mother had groomed her for, even if the thought of doing so without her was one she couldn't even contemplate.

Jagged glass lined her throat. *Baby steps*, she told herself, swallowing hard. She could do this. She just needed to take baby steps. And guard against her feelings for Nico while she did it because her instinctive response to him last night had revealed too much.

She wasn't a teenager anymore in the throes of a wicked crush, overwhelmed by a sexual attraction she'd had no hope of fighting. The connection she and Nico had shared hadn't been special as she'd thought it had been. He'd killed any romantic illusions she'd had about him dead the night he'd slept with another woman and made it clear they were over.

That she still found him compelling was an indication of her weakness when it came to him, one she needed to stamp out dead now that she was back in New York.

Because like it or not, he *was* her boss. The man who could green-light or kill her dream. Either she could keep fighting that fact, fighting *him* as she had been for the past six months, or she could prove him wrong. And since launching Vivre in time for Christmas, preserving her legacy, was all that mattered, her decision was clear.

Her first step was to dust herself off after her disastrous performance last night and make her first day back in New York a success.

A determined fire lighting her blood, she dressed in her most stylish cherry-colored suit, walked to work amid the crisp autumn glory and spent the morning meeting with Giorgio about Vivre.

She was excited to discover the splashy Christmas launch in Times Square she had planned was doable, but the tight deadlines to complete the advertising campaign made her head spin. It meant she would have to have her celebrities secured within the next week, their advertising spots filmed shortly thereafter, which might actually be impossible given how slow those things worked.

But it was doable. She focused on that as she spent the rest of the day nailing down the details Nico had requested so he would have nothing to question when she presented him with the revised plan. Then she took Mireille out for dinner at Tempesta Di Fuoco, Stefan Bianco's hot spot in Chelsea, as she turned her attention to her most pressing issue.

Celebrities were her sister's world. Socially connected in a way Chloe had never been with her sparkling, extroverted personality and undeniable beauty that mirrored their mother's icy blonde looks, there were few people Mireille didn't know in Manhattan.

Her sister refused to talk business until they had exotic martinis sitting in front of them. "All right," she said, sitting back with her drink in hand. "Tell me about the campaign."

Chloe cradled her glass between her fingers. "It's about an authentic beauty, as you know. About expressing your true colors. But we're approaching it from a different point of view with each perfume. One, for example, is about moving past your physical limitations. Another about incorporating a difficult past as part of what makes you unique. *Irreplaceable*."

"I love it," said Mireille, looking intrigued. "It's brilliant. Give me your list."

Chloe took a deep breath. "Number one. Carrie Taylor." The supermodel had made it big as a plus-size model and was gracing the cover of every magazine on the newsstands.

Mireille cocked a brow. "You aren't reaching high, are you?"

"I told you I was. Second is Lashaunta." A pop singer who had recently had a string of chart-topping records, she had forged a successful career despite a prominent scar on her face. Or perhaps *because* of it, as it gave her such a distinctive look.

"Next?"

"Desdemona Parker." A world-class athlete, she'd made it to the top of her sport despite the inherited disease that had nearly ended her career. "And finally," Chloe concluded, "Eddie Carello for our men's fragrance."

Mireille blinked. "You're kidding."

"He's a survivor," Chloe said quietly. "He grew up in the projects. He perfectly embodies the spirit of Soar."

Mireille let out a husky laugh. "I can see why Nico cut you down to size. He's not wrong about the brand taking a hit. It isn't going to be an easy sell. Do you have backups?"

Chloe listed them. "But I need my A list. It's Nico's nonnegotiable."

Her sister pursed her lips. "I can help with Lashaunta and Carrie. You're out of luck with Desdemona and Eddie, however. Eddie is near untouchable, he's too hot right now. Desdemona, I have no connections to, and neither does anyone in our PR department. We're not big in sports."

Chloe's face fell.

"Lazzero, however," her sister mused, "might be able to help. I read in the paper this morning Eddie is attending the launch party for Blaze, Lazzero's new running shoe, at Di Fiore's tomorrow night. Desdemona has an endorsement deal with Supersonic. She might be there, too."

Chloe chewed on her lip. Her father had been godfather to all the Di Fiore brothers when his good friend Leone had died, including Nico's middle brother, Lazzero, and youngest, Santo. But only Nico had ended up at Evolution after her father had taken him on as his protégé. Lazzero and Santo had put themselves through school on sports scholarships, going on to found one of the hottest sportswear companies on the planet in Supersonic, with an investment from Martino to help them along.

Chloe's lashes lowered. "I wanted to do this by myself. To prove to Nico I can."

"Lazzero is not cheating. Lazzero is being *resourceful*."

Chloe tapped her fingernails on the table. "Do you think he'd let us attend the party?"

"There's only one way to find out." Mireille picked up her phone and made the call.

"Lazzero, darling," she purred. "I need you."

Whatever was said on the other end of the phone made her laugh. "I do so call you just to chat. But right now, Chloe and I need a favor. We need an invite to your party tomorrow night to chat up Eddie Carello and Desdemona Parker for an influencer deal."

Mireille frowned at Lazzero's response. "Oh, she isn't? That's too bad. Eddie is, though, right?"

Chloe's stomach dropped. *No Desdemona.*

Mireille nodded at whatever Lazzero said in response. "It won't be me, I have plans. It will be Chloe. And I will pass the message on. You are, as usual, a doll."

Chloe eyed her as she signed off. "What did he say?"

"Desdemona is out of town, but he's emailing me and her agent and making the introduction. As for the party, it's a yes. He'll leave your name at the door." A wicked smile curved her sister's lips. "He said to wear a short dress. Eddie likes legs."

And so that was how Chloe found herself the following night passing her credentials to the big lug in a dark suit at the door of Di Fiore's, the upscale bar in midtown Manhattan Lazzero and Santo ran as part of their sports conglomerate.

Clad in the very short, rose-gold dress Mireille had lent her and surrounded by the trendy crowd, Chloe felt hopelessly out of place.

"You can come this way," said the lug, plucking Chloe out of the lineup and ushering her through a side door and into the party that was already in full swing. There he handed her over to a hostess who led her through a crush of people to where Lazzero held court at the bar. He was supremely sophisticated all in black. Chloe had always found his hawk-like profile and dark eyes highly intimidating. Unlike Nico, who had intrigued her from the very beginning with his quiet, serious demeanor—as if the weight of the world had been placed on his shoulders.

Lazzero, however, made an effort to put her at ease, handing her a glass of wine and chatting idly with her about what she and Mireille were up to. Having not had time to eat, Chloe felt the wine go straight to her head, making the crowd seem much less unapproachable.

After a few minutes, Lazzero nodded toward the end of the bar. "Eddie at three o'clock."

Her pulse gave a flutter as she turned to find the famous bad-boy actor lounging his lean, rangy, jean-clad body against the bar while a group of rather exquisite women attempted to capture his attention. Her stomach fell. How was she supposed to compete with that?

She turned back to Lazzero. Ran a self-conscious hand over her hair. She wasn't going to get another opportunity like this. She just had to *do* it. "Do I look okay?"

His dark eyes glittered with amusement. "Affirmative. Ten minutes, Chloe. That's all you've got. I have a rule at my parties—no one hassles you. It makes them want to come back."

She moistened her lips. "Got it."

He eyed her. "Are you sure you want to do this? He's a bit of a piece of work."

"Yes."

He pressed another glass of wine into her hand. "Go."

Chloe took a sip of the wine, sucked in a deep breath and started walking, forcing herself to trace a straight line toward the actor before she chickened out. The girls around him looked down their noses at her as she approached. Used to this treatment when she was with Mireille, Chloe ignored them, walked right up to Eddie and stuck out her hand. "Eddie, I'm Chloe Russo. My family and I own Evolution. I'd like to talk to you about a fragrance I've developed with you in mind."

The actor swept his gaze over her dismissively, before he got to her legs, where he lingered. "Who did you say you are?" he queried absentmindedly.

Chloe repeated her spiel, refusing to give in to the knots tying themselves in her stomach.

Eddie lifted his slumberous dark gaze to hers. Flicked the girl off the stool beside him. "Have a seat."

Nico pointed his car home, a brutally hard day of meetings behind him. A beer and the hot tub at his penthouse beckoned, but so did a phone call with his brothers at the end of the day. Old habits died hard, and checking in with Lazzero and Santo to make sure their world was upright was one of them.

It had been that way ever since their father's company had imploded when Nico was a teenager, his father and his marriage along with it, leaving Nico as the last line of defense between his family and the street when his mother had walked out. When life as you'd known it had dissolved once beneath your feet, you made sure it never happened again.

He punched Lazzero's cell into his hands-free. It rang five times before his brother picked up, the sound of music pulsing in the background.

"Sorry." The music faded as Lazzero moved to a quieter spot. "It's our Blaze launch tonight."

Nico rubbed a palm against his temple. "*Mi dispiace.* I just walked out of my last meeting minutes ago."

"No worries." An amused note flavored his brother's lazy drawl. "You didn't tell me you were sending your little bird my way."

"My little bird?"

"Chloe. She's here chatting up Eddie Carello for some sponsorship deal."

Nico blinked at the bright headlights of an oncoming car. "*Chloe* is there chatting up Eddie Carello?"

"And doing a pretty good job of it I might say. Must be the dress. I told her he likes legs."

Nico brought his back teeth together. "Shut it down, Lazzero. You know better than that. She's no match for him."

More of that patented male amusement in his brother's voice. "She looks like a match for him to me. She has his *undivided* attention at the moment."

"Lazzero," Nico growled. "Shut it down."

"Gotta go," his brother apologized. "A client just arrived. You should drop by."

Nico swore a blue streak, yanked the steering wheel around and did an overtly illegal U-turn. Approaching celebrities was the PR department's job. He was already feeling guilty about the board meeting and the necessarily harsh lesson he'd administered to Chloe. She was so vulnerable despite that sharp mouth of hers. But it had seemed to do the trick of jolting her out of that frozen state she'd been in, and for that, he'd considered it a success.

She did, however, need to be treated with kid gloves at the moment. She was the key to Evolution's success. She had to *believe* she could take her mother's place. But the question mark with Chloe had always been her confidence. Her belief in herself.

It didn't seem to be lacking, however, as Nico strode into Di Fiore's to find Lazzero romancing a tall blonde at the bar and Chloe doing the same with the most notorious womanizer in Hollywood.

Her dark hair shone loose around her lovely face, the champagne-colored dress she wore as she sat perched on the high stool highlighting every dip and curve of her slim, perfect figure. Her legs—and there was a lot of them—were a jaw-dropping, toned work of art. They made his mouth go dry.

And that was before he got to those gorgeous eyes of hers—dark rippling pools framed by the longest, most luxurious lashes he'd ever seen. Eyes that had once made him lose his common sense. He thought maybe she'd put about ten coats of mascara on.

Carello had one hand on his jean-clad thigh, the other around his drink, talking in an animated fashion while Chloe listened, her clear, bright laughter cutting through the din of the crowd.

Nico's mouth tightened as the actor slid his arm to the back of her stool and moved in closer.

Resisting the urge to walk over there and pluck her off the stool, he lifted his hand and signaled the bartender instead. The young hipster called out a greeting to him and slid his favorite dark ale across the bar.

"You thought that was a good idea?" he growled as Lazzero lost the blonde and ambled over.

His brother hiked a shoulder. "I'm not her babysitter. You are. How you found yourself in that role is beyond me."

"You know full well how I did. Martino made it impossible to say no."

Lazzero took a sip of his beer. Eyed him. "When are you going to tell her about his cancer? It would make your life easier, you know."

It would. But Martino had made him promise not to tell his girls about the rare form of cancer that would have eventually claimed his life. He'd asked Nico to take care of them instead by taking his place at the helm of the company and ensuring it prospered. Telling Chloe now would only add to the emotional upheaval she was going through. And quite frankly, he needed her head on the job.

He threw back a swig of his beer. Wiped his mouth. "I have no idea why Martino even thought this was a good idea."

"Maybe because you did such a good job with Santo and me," Lazzero goaded. "We are such model citizens."

"I am questioning that right now." Nico slid his attention back to Carello. Watched him put a palm on Chloe's bare thigh. She didn't flinch, throwing her hair back over her shoulder and laughing at whatever he said.

Heat seared his belly. "How much has she had to drink?"

"Enough to boost her confidence." Lazzero leaned a hip against the bar. Slid an assessing gaze over him. "Tough day?"

"Evolution's stock is in the toilet, we desperately need a hit product and Giorgio has been executing an internal smear campaign against me. It's been a joy."

Lazzero's mouth curled. "He is a nuisance. He's not a serious threat."

But he was distracting him at a time he couldn't

afford to be distracted. When Evolution was tee-
tering on the edge of a defining moment. And
that, he couldn't have.

A tall, lanky male with razed blond hair pushed
through the crowd to the bar, leaning over to say
something to Eddie. The actor gave Chloe a re-
gretful look, then said something that made her
face fall, then brighten as Carello took something
out of his wallet and slid it onto the bar.

Nico's fingers tightened around his beer bottle
as the actor bent and pressed a kiss to each of
Chloe's cheeks, staining her skin with two twin
spots of pink. Then he and his entourage headed
off through the crowd.

A surge of triumph filled Chloe as she sat holding
Eddie Carello's agent's business card, his parting
words ringing in her ears. *Call my agent. Give
him the details. Tell him I gave this the green
light if he's good with it.*

She shook her head bemusedly. Slid off the bar
stool, a half-finished glass of champagne in her
hand. The world rocked ever so slightly beneath
her feet. She'd never had much of a head for alcohol, but Eddie had insisted on that glass of cham-

pagne, and OMG, he'd just said yes. Never in her wildest dreams had she imagined he would.

Untouchable, my foot.

She turned and headed for Lazzero to thank him. Pulled up short. Nico was standing beside his brother at the bar, the jacket of his dark suit discarded, a drink in his hand.

Her pulse went haywire. Why did that happen every time? And why did he look so good in a shirt and tie? The tie loosened, his hair ruffled, he looked younger, like he had when they'd first met. *Devastating.*

But *that* Nico didn't exist, she reminded herself, heart thumping against her chest like a bass drum. And she'd do well to remember it.

She straightened her shoulders and walked the length of the bar to where the two men stood. Lazzero waved off her thanks and melted into the crowd to greet someone. Nico set that penetrating gray gaze of his on her.

"I told you to *secure* him. Meaning use the PR department. Not take on Hollywood yourself."

She lifted a shoulder. "The PR department didn't have access to him. Mireille said he was untouchable. So we asked Lazzero for help."

He leaned back against the bar, his free hand crossed in the crook of his folded elbow. "What did he say?"

A victorious smile played at the corners of her mouth. It might have been her best moment ever. "He said yes."

His eyes widened. "He did?"

"Yes. But," she qualified, "it's contingent on his agent's approval."

Nico's gaze warmed with a glimmer of something that might have been admiration. "I'm impressed. How did you convince him?"

"I explained the campaign to him. Why he was the inspiration for Soar. He was flattered—said he liked the idea of having a fragrance created for him. It turns out," she concluded thoughtfully, "that men are true to their biology. They like to have their egos stroked. It's their Achilles' heel."

A hint of a smile played at his mouth. "That may be true," he acknowledged. "But Carello is not to be played with. His reputation precedes him. Get his agent to sign off, then leave him the hell alone."

"I *know* that." Irritation burrowed a bumpy red path beneath her skin. "That's why I told him I had a boyfriend. Honestly, Nico, do you think I'm a total neophyte?"

"Sometimes I do, yes."

She made a sound at the back of her throat. "Well, you can go home now. The show's over. Your babysitting duties are officially done for the night."

He nodded toward her glass. "Finish that and I'll drive you home."

Oh, no. She was not having him shepherd her home like some stray sheep who'd wandered into the wrong field. She had conquered tonight, and she was leaving under her own steam. Because, truthfully, all she wanted was a hot shower and her bed now that the world had blissfully right-sided itself.

She lifted her chin. "I'm not ready to leave. It was so nice of Lazzero to invite me. It's a great party. There's dancing and everything. I think I'll stay."

He set his silvery gaze on hers. "Let's go dance, then."

Her heart tripped over itself. She knew how good it felt to be that close to all that muscle and masculinity. How *exciting* it was, because he'd subjected her to its full effects before he'd cast her aside and chosen another.

"I didn't say I wanted to dance right *now*." She held up her half-finished glass of champagne. "I still have this."

"I think you've had enough." He plucked the glass out of her fingers, captured her wrist in his hand and was leading her through the crowd toward the packed dance floor before she could voice an objection. She knew it for the bad idea it was before they'd even gotten there. Eddie had touched her bare thigh and hadn't even caused a ripple. Nico's fingers wrapped around her wrist were like a surge of electricity through her entire body. She felt it right to the tips of her toes.

But then they'd reached the mosaic-tiled dance floor with its elegant chandelier. With a smooth flick of his wrist, Nico tugged her to him. A little more pressure and she was firmly within the circle of his arms, shielded from the other dancers by his height and breadth.

One of her hands in his, the other resting on his waist, it wasn't a close hold. But this was Nico. Every inch of her skin heated as it came into whisper-soft contact with his tall, powerful body. And then the scent of him kicked in, filling her head and electrifying her senses.

Smoky and elusive, it was pure, understated sensuality. Vetiver, the warm Indian grass known for its earthy, hedonistic appeal her mother had highlighted in Voluttuoso, her final fragrance. Chloe had always thought it was sexy. On Nico, with his overt virility and intensely masculine scent, it was knee weakening.

One dance. She kept her gaze riveted to the knot of his elegant silver tie. Unfortunately for her, the song was a jazzy, sexy tune, in keeping with the über-cool vibe of the party. A smooth, instinctive dancer, Nico was an excellent lead, guiding her steps easily in the small space they had carved out with a light pressure on her palm.

It should have been simple to exercise the mind control her yoga instructor was always preaching. Instead, her thoughts flew back to that sultry Fourth of July night that changed everything.

Her in Nico's arms…the illicit, forbidden passion that had burst into flames between them… how for the first time in her life, she'd felt truly, completely alive.

She lifted her gaze to his, searched for some

indication that everything they'd shared hadn't been the imaginings of her eighteen-year-old mind. That she'd *meant* something to him like she'd thought she had. But his cool gray gaze was focused on her with a calculating intensity that sent that irrational, naive hope plunging to the bottom of her heart.

"We started off on the wrong foot the other night," he murmured. "We need to work as a team, Chloe, *together*, not apart, if we have any hope of preserving what your parents built. Full-out warfare is not going to work."

She arched a brow at him. "Is that an apology?"

"If you like," he said evenly. "Like it or not, we are in this together. We succeed or fail together. You decide which it is."

Her lashes lowered. "I agree we need a better working relationship. But this is my company, Nico. You need to listen to me, too. You can't just run roughshod over me with that insatiable need for control of yours. I *know* what's going to make Evolution a success. There's no doubt in my mind it's Vivre."

"Put the rest of the pieces of the plan in place and I might agree. And," he said, inclining his head, "I promise to listen more. *If* you stop trying to bait me at every turn."

Her mouth twisted. "A truce, then?"

A mocking glint filled his gaze. "A truce. We can celebrate by attending the Palm Beach fund-raiser together. It will present a very public united front."

Her parents' favorite fund-raiser. A glittering, star-studded musical event in Palm Beach every year in support of breast cancer—a disease her mother's best friend had succumbed to. Her stomach did a nervous dip at the thought of attending it with Nico.

She tipped her head back to look up at him. "You mean you don't have one of your hot dates lined up for it?"

Hot in the sense they never lasted with Nico. She wasn't sure she'd ever seen him photographed with the same woman twice.

"I haven't had a hot date in six months," he drawled. "It will have to wait until Evolution isn't in danger of falling through the cracks."

A calculated insult intended to remind her of her irresponsibility and his immutable focus.

"However will you survive?" she goaded, skin stinging.

"I will *manage*," he murmured, eyes on hers. "Careful, Chloe, we've barely gotten this cease-fire of ours under way."

She sank her teeth into her lip. At the erotic image that one word inserted into her head. It took very little of her imagination to wonder what he would look like in the shower satisfying that physical need, his beautiful body primed for release.

She closed her eyes. She *hated* him. This was insanity.

The song finished. She stepped hastily out of his arms, smoothing her dress down over her hips. Nico gave her a pointed look. "Ready to leave?"

The concrete set of his jaw said there was no point arguing. He wasn't leaving her here. He would wait all night if he had to because this was Nico—relentless in everything he did. Patient like the most tenacious predator in achieving what he wanted.

"Yes," she agreed with a helpless sigh.

He placed a palm to her back as they wound

their way through the crowd to say good-night to Lazzero. The heat of it fizzled over her skin, warming her layers deep, a real-life chemical reaction she'd never been able to defuse.

It rendered her silent on the trip home, the warm, luxurious interior of the car wrapping her in a sleek, dark cocoon as they slipped through quiet streets. She was so tired as Nico walked her to her door, she stumbled with the key as she tried to push it into the lock.

His fingers brushed against hers as he collected the keys from her hand and unlocked the door. Little pinpricks of heat exploded across her skin, a surge of warmth staining her cheeks as she looked up at him to thank him. Found herself all caught up in his smoky gaze that suddenly seemed to have a charge in it that stalled the breath in her throat.

"Go inside and go to bed, Chloe," he said huskily. "And lock the door."

His intention ever since he'd walked into that bar tonight, she reminded herself, past her spinning head. To prevent her from slipping into Eddie Carello's hands.

She slicked her tongue across suddenly dry

lips. Cocked her chin at a defiant angle. "Mission accomplished. I'll be in bed by midnight. But then again, you always get what you want, don't you, Nico?"

His gray gaze was heavy-lidded as it focused on her mouth for an infinitesimal pause. "Not always," he said quietly.

Then he disappeared into the night.

CHAPTER THREE

IT HAD BEEN the champagne talking. Chloe convinced herself of that version of events as she walked to work the next morning. That cryptic comment from Nico on her doorstep, the chemistry that had seemed so palpable between them. Because not once in all the years since their summer flirtation had he ever looked at her like that.

She'd merely been a blip on his radar. A casual diversion he'd regretted when more sophisticated choices had come along. Thinking it had been any more than that would make her a fool where he was concerned and she'd stopped being that a long time ago.

Whatever misguided sense of duty he was displaying toward her, this *power trip* he was on, Nico's ambition was the only thing he cared about, a fact she would do well to remember. She'd agreed to this truce of theirs only for the greater good of the company. Because saving Evolution was all that mattered.

She perfected her spiel for Eddie's agent as she rode the elevator to her office, said good-morning to Clara, whom she'd decided was not only witty but astonishingly efficient, and took the messages her assistant handed her into her office.

Done in antiques, with a Louis XVI writing desk and chairs, ultra-feminine lace-edged, silk curtains and warm lamp lighting, the office that had once been her mother's wrapped itself around her like a whisper-soft memory. But her mind was all business as she picked up the phone and called Eddie's agent. A good thing, too, because when she reached him, he told her he was on his way out of town but could have lunch that day before he left.

Apprehensive Eddie would change his mind if it waited, Chloe jumped on the invitation. Unfortunately, his agent wasn't immediately sold on the endorsement, but in the end he relented, only because Eddie seemed so keen on the project and the actor had a movie coming out at Christmas, just as the massive campaign for Soar would appear.

Chloe floated back to the office and announced her victory to Mireille, who was just as excited as she.

"*I*," she informed Chloe, "have good news and bad news for you. The good news is that Lashaunta is interested. She loves the campaign. It really resonated with her."

Chloe's heart soared. Lashaunta was a megastar. "That's *amazing*."

"The bad news is that Carrie Taylor is a no. She's about to represent a competing fragrance. Desdemona," she concluded, "I'm still working on."

Which meant they needed to secure their plan B supermodel, Estelle Markov, for Nico to give them the green light. He might approve the plan with only three of their four celebrities in place, but any less than that and Chloe knew she'd be out of luck.

While Mireille worked on Estelle, Chloe went off to put the final piece of her buzz campaign into effect, personally delivering samples of the Vivre fragrances to each and every Evolution employee's desk, explaining the story behind the perfumes. A streak of the devil possessing her, she also had Clara courier samples of the fragrances to the board members, making sure she also sent one for their significant other.

She *would* win them over.

Hurricane Chloe had entered the building.

A wry smile tugged at Nico's lips as he waved Chloe into his office late on Friday afternoon and motioned for her to take a seat as he finished up a conference call.

She walked to the window instead, vibrating with the perpetual energy she'd been displaying all week in her very effective campaign to prove him wrong. Her slender body encased in a soft, off-white sweater, dark jeans tucked into knee-high boots and a fawn-colored jacket topping it off, she wore her hair in a high ponytail, her flawless skin bare of makeup.

The hard kick she administered to his solar plexus wasn't unexpected. He'd been fighting his attraction to Chloe ever since the first moment he'd set foot in the Russo household and eyes on Martino and Juliette's eldest daughter.

Twenty to Chloe's sixteen, he'd been hard and bitter from his experiences. But something about the quiet, passionate Chloe had penetrated his close-packed outer shell. Perhaps he had recognized a piece of himself in her—the need they had both had to bury themselves behind their layers to protect themselves against the world. Perhaps it had been how she had sold her subtle beauty short when he'd always found her far more attractive than her stunning sister.

He'd told himself he couldn't have her. That he would never put his position as Martino's protégé in jeopardy—the career that had meant everything to him as he'd finally built a solid footing under his feet. Until unintended and explosive, the attraction between him and Chloe had slipped his reins at the Russo's annual Fourth of July party.

Martino, who'd witnessed the kiss, had brought him up short, asking his intentions when it came to his daughter. Pursue Chloe seriously or leave her alone, he had said, knowing what Nico *was*—a man who would never trust, never commit to a woman because of the scars his early life had left behind.

So he'd walked away. Done it the hard way so it would be a clean break. So he wouldn't be tempted with what he couldn't have. Because Martino had been right—he would have broken Chloe's heart far worse than he had in the end.

Martino might not be alive, he conceded, studying the delicate length of her spine, and Chloe wasn't a teenager anymore, but he had a new responsibility now. To protect her, not bed her. To nurture her as Martino had asked of him. It was a promise he would not break.

His call with the West Coast team over, he pushed out of his chair and walked to where she stood at the window. She turned, her face expectant. "Did you look at the plan?"

"Yes." He glanced at his watch. "I have time to go through it before my dinner plans if you'd like."

When she answered in the affirmative, he strode out to reception, sent his PA, Simone, home, then returned to pour himself a Scotch. When Chloe refused his offer of a drink, he joined her in the lounge, where she stood at the windows, enjoying the view.

Designed to work and entertain with its Italian glass chandeliers, dining room for ten and magnificent vista of a night-lit Central Park, the view was Nico's favorite thing about the space he spent far too much time in.

Chloe turned around. "So what did you think?"

"I think you've made a very persuasive case for Vivre being the Christmas focus. The plan is excellent." A wry smile touched his mouth. "It was also impossible," he conceded drily, "to miss your blitz campaign. Very clever. I couldn't walk the halls without hearing about it. Simone can't stop raving about Be. Jerry Schumacher called me this morning to beg for an early production bottle for his wife."

A tiny smile curved her mouth at the mention of Evolution's most senior board member. "I did say I would win them over. But more important," she added, excitement filling her voice, "the media is raving about Vivre, Nico. The editor of the most influential fashion magazine in America is crazy about Soar. She wants to feature it as her must-have product for Christmas. I think it's going to be a huge hit."

He held up a hand before she got too carried away. "I saw that. I do, however, still have real concerns about the timing. It seems inordinately tight. I want more than Giorgio's rose-colored glasses making this decision."

"It is a tight timeline," she admitted. "I may not sleep. But we can do it. The advertising space is booked, and all four of our celebrities have the time in their schedule to film the spots."

He addressed the one glaring hole in the plan. "I don't see Carrie Taylor in there. What happened to her?"

She sank her teeth into her lip. "She's representing a competing fragrance. But Mireille has a verbal commitment from Estelle Markov, who's making it big in Europe. I think she'll be perfect to target that audience."

"I've never heard of her." He frowned. "She doesn't have Carrie Taylor's cachet, Chloe. Nor is the European market anywhere near the size of the North American one."

"But she's amazing." Her eyes shimmered with fire. "When was the last time you were a twentysomething fashionista with breasts?"

A dry look back. "Point taken."

"Not to mention the fact that Eddie and Lashaunta could carry this campaign on their own if they had to," she plunged on. "Carrie is not a make-or-break for us."

He took a sip of his Scotch. Considered his options. The skincare line he had favored was, in truth, not going to set the world on fire. It would, however, provide very solid profits. Vivre might be that superstar product line Evolution so desperately needed, but was he insane to bet the company on it?

"This is a *fifty-million-dollar* campaign," he said, fixing his gaze on Chloe's. "We've never done anything of this magnitude before. It needs to be executed flawlessly—right down to the last detail. Needs to put Evolution on everyone's lips again. Are you *sure* you can get it into market in time?"

"Yes." Her head bobbed up and down. "Trust me, Nico. I can do this."

He gave her a long look. "Okay," he said finally, pointing his glass at her. "Let's do it, then."

The world tilted beneath Chloe's feet. "Did you just say yes?"

He smiled. *"Si."*

"Why?"

"Because I believe in you," he said quietly. "You're a brilliant scientist, Chloe. Juliette said you have even better instincts than she had at this age. That you have the *magic* in you. I just wasn't sure you or Vivre was ready."

Hot tears prickled beneath her eyelids. A knot she hadn't been conscious of unraveled in her chest. Three years of blood, sweat and tears. Six months of praying she had created something that would do her mother proud. To be so close to watching her dream reach fruition almost undid her.

But there was also *fear*. Her stomach clenched hard at the responsibility that now lay on her shoulders, icy tentacles of apprehension sinking into her skin. What if she failed? What if she'd been overly optimistic and couldn't get the campaign into market in time? What if she was wrong about Vivre? What if it wasn't going to be the smash hit she thought it would be?

She inhaled a deep breath. Steadied herself. She wasn't wrong. She knew it in her heart. She just wished her mother was here to tell her that. To be the second half of her she had always been. Instead, she had to do this herself.

"I know this is the right path for Evolution," she said huskily. "I can feel it in my bones."

Nico nodded. "Then let me give you a few additional thoughts I have."

They sat at the table in the dining room and worked through the plan. Released one by one in limited-edition launches in the weeks leading up to Christmas, the campaign for Vivre was all about buzz building and creating a sense of exclusivity for the perfumes.

Vivre's four celebrity ambassadors would do exclusive appearances at the Times Square pop-up retail location in conjunction with the massive promotional campaign that would blanket the globe, intensifying the buzz.

Nico frowned as he looked at the timeline. "When does Eddie's movie come out?"

"The second week of December." Chloe pointed to the date on the timeline. "That's why we're launching Soar that week."

"What are you doing on his side of things to cross-promote?"

She pursed her lips. "I hadn't gotten that far yet."

"You should do something with the theaters.

Hand samples out. Put the fragrance in the gift bags at the premieres. Run the campaign on theater screens."

So smart. She tapped her coffee mug against her chin. "I don't know if we have time."

He lifted a brow.

"We'll make it happen," she corrected hastily. "No problem."

He offered a half dozen more brilliant ideas before they were done, Chloe frantically scribbling notes. She had to reluctantly admit by the time they were finished that while she and her uncle had created an inspired plan, Nico had taken it to a whole other level with his innate sense of timing and brilliant business instincts.

Which had never been in question, she brooded as he got up from the table to shrug on an elegant black dinner jacket. Her father would never have taken him on as his protégé if he hadn't possessed Leone Di Fiore's uncanny sense of financial wizardry. What she couldn't forgive was how Nico had taken advantage of the trust her father had placed in him with what Giorgio had described as a systematic campaign to gain power.

She had always believed Nico operated by a

rigid code of honor instilled in him by the adversity he'd faced in his younger years. Until he'd slept with Angelique Dubois to seal a deal and she'd seen how far his ambition could drive him.

A painful wound echoed down low. Unfortunately, it didn't diminish her physical awareness of him one bit. He did formal better than any man she'd ever known—the exquisitely cut black dinner jacket accentuating his broad shoulders, the dark pants molding his powerful thighs, the white shirt and black bow tie casting his startling good looks into harsh relief. He was so intensely virile he made her stomach flip.

Clearly he had much more exciting plans than she for tonight. In his life that didn't include hot dates.

"There is," he murmured, returning to lounge against the table, "a condition to my saying yes to the plan."

Her stomach fell. *Not another hoop to jump through.*

She pushed out of the chair and stood to meet him on even ground. "Which is?" she prompted, tipping her head back to look up at him, prepared to do whatever she needed to do to make this happen.

"The company is suffering without a visible creative force. Everyone responsible for the future of the company is looking for a sign the magic is still there—that it didn't disappear along with your mother." He pointed his Scotch at her. "You and I both know it didn't, but that's not good enough."

Her stomach dropped right to the floor this time. "What are you asking me to do?"

"The company needs a face, Chloe. Vivre, with its massive promotional campaign, is the perfect opportunity to position you as the creative force behind the company. The heir apparent. To tell your story. But we can't do that if you're holed up in the lab."

The knot that had begun to unravel twisted itself back into place. "No, Nico. Don't ask me to do this. Not now."

"It has to be now." He lifted a shoulder, a sympathetic gleam in his eyes. "I wanted to put it off. To give you more time to find your feet, but I can't do that if I'm betting the bank on you. On Vivre. It would be irresponsible of me. But I promise you, I will be there by your side every step of the way."

Old demons mixed with the apprehension climbing her throat. With the pressure, too much pressure, that had been heaped on her for months. *Forever.* It rose up inside her, pushing at the edges of the tightly held composure she'd been clinging to for weeks.

"I am not my mother," she said, a raw edge to her voice. "She was larger than life, Nico. She had incredible charisma. I don't have that kind of a story to tell."

"I'm not asking you to be her," he countered. "I'm asking you to be *you*, Chloe. You created your own signature fragrance at *seventeen* that sold like wildfire. How is that not a great story to tell?"

"It's not the same thing."

"How is it different?" He shook his head, mouth flattening into a straight line. "This is your Achilles' heel, I get that. You've never been comfortable in the spotlight. You don't think you can live up to this image you have of your mother and Mireille, so you hide yourself away in the lab, when what you really need to be is comfortable in your own skin."

The oh-so-accurate assessment hit her square in the chest. She *knew* her weaknesses. This, however, was not one she had the bandwidth to deal with right now.

"You would regret it," she told him. "I am a loose cannon with the press. They start firing questions at me and I freeze. Put a camera in front of me and I'm worse. I can't answer a question, let alone articulate a vision."

"You will improve. You'll have the best training available."

She bit her lip. "I can't do it."

"You *won't* do it," he corrected harshly. "This isn't about you anymore, Chloe. It's about a company we're trying to save together."

"No, I can't." She clenched her hands into fists, the band around her chest tightening until she felt like she couldn't breathe. "I know what I'm supposed to be, Nico. I've spent my life trying to live up to that. I have given you Vivre, what I know will be a smash hit. But what you're asking of me now is too much."

"Why?" Harsh, implacable.

Because if she stepped into her mother's shoes, she would have to admit she was gone. She would have to acknowledge a pain so deep it might shatter her into pieces and she might never be able to put herself back together again. Because she was barely hanging on as it was.

Heat lashed the backs of her eyes, swift and unrelenting. She walked unsteadily to the window, where she stood staring out at a glorious amber-and-yellow-painted Central Park.

"Chloe," Nico said huskily, closing his hands around her shoulders. She shrugged, attempted to jerk out of his hold, but he sank his fingers deeper into her flesh and turned her around to face him.

"I know you can do this," he murmured, fixing his gaze on hers. "You just have to *believe* you can do it."

The dark, sensual scent of him wrapped itself around her. An irresistible wall of heat that drew her in a way she didn't want to acknowledge, he was overwhelmingly solid in a world that seemed to have dissolved around the edges. She knew she should look away, put some distance between them, because he was the last man on earth she should be drawn to in that way. But she couldn't seem to do it.

His eyes darkened. Electric currents vibrated the air between them as he lifted a hand to stroke his thumb along the line of her jaw. The tension coiling her insides snaked tighter, caging her breath in her lungs.

Walk away, Chloe. It was the smart thing to do. Why, then, would her feet not seem to move?

A discreet cough cut across the charge in the air. Her pulse beat a jagged edge at her throat as she stepped back, inordinately grateful for the distraction. Pivoting, she took in the elegant blonde standing in the doorway.

Nico's date, she assumed. Who was one of the most beautiful women Chloe had ever laid eyes on. Shoulder-length blond hair cut into a sleek bob, curvaceous figure clad in a sapphire-blue beaded dress she wore with sky-high heels, she was undeniably his type.

Turning on that effortless charm of his, Nico asked *Helene* to give them a minute. Chloe turned back to face him as the blonde retreated to reception. "Your *nonhot* date?"

"The president of Germany's largest department store chain," Nico corrected. "She has a thing for Mario Conti. He's doing *Tosca* at the Met tonight."

"And you are solidifying that relationship." She lifted her chin as an ancient hurt lashed her insides. "A specialty of yours."

His gaze narrowed, razor-sharp, as it rested on hers. "The Source Minerale deal was signed a month before my relationship with Angelique began, Chloe. So whatever your list of my faults, you can take sleeping my way to the top off it."

A rush of color stained her cheeks. She tugged her lip between her teeth, caught utterly flat-footed. "It was everywhere in the papers, Nico."

"The announcement was strategically timed to coincide with a key anniversary for Source Minerale. The deal, however, was done way before then." His mouth curved in a mocking smile as he crossed the room to his desk. "Don't lose any sleep over it. I'm sure you'll find at least half a dozen of my other failings to cling to."

Her skin stung from the rebuke. She watched as he dumped a sheaf of papers into his briefcase. Considered this new piece of information. If Nico had not slept with Angelique to seal the

Source Minerale deal just days after they had shared that passionate encounter at the Fourth of July party, it could only mean his preference for the beautiful Angelique had dictated his actions.

A low throb pulsed inside her where his betrayal still lived. Clearly what they'd shared had always meant far more to her than it had to him, and she needed, once and for all, to realize that, instead of thinking he was something he wasn't. Instead of imagining *moments* between them like that one just now that weren't real.

Nico snapped his briefcase shut. Set a level gaze on her. "We have a deal, then?"

She lifted her chin. "You're leaving me no choice. But I guess you know that." She scooped up her things and stalked to the door. "Enjoy your evening. Apparently, Mario Conti brings down the house."

Mario Conti did bring down the house in the first half of *Tosca* at the stately, always magnificent Metropolitan Opera House. Puccini's dramatic story of love, lust and murder against a backdrop of the politics of soon-to-be Napoleon's Rome was spectacular, with Conti playing the opera's protagonist, the doomed Angelotti, to perfection.

But Nico's mind was on Chloe instead of the moving performance, and her high emotion as she'd stormed out of his office. Had he pushed her off the edge of the cliff with his demand she be the face of Evolution? Was it too much pressure for her to handle?

He was also, he acknowledged, as Conti took an extended bow, annoyed with her and with himself for letting her goad him into dredging up ancient history in Angelique. Because he'd hurt her again. He'd seen it in her face. And perhaps, in hindsight, ending things like that between them might not have been the right way to go about it. But he'd been young, his emotional IQ not yet fully developed.

His honor, however, he fumed inwardly, had never been in question. And that was what annoyed him most of all. If it hadn't been for his *honor*, he would have taken everything Chloe had been offering that night. Which would have been a disaster for them both.

The standing ovation complete, he escorted Helene to the bar for a drink. While she went to the powder room, he installed himself at the bar. Attempted to right-side his mood. But the bar was jam-packed, which left him cooling his heels with ancient memories of that night with Chloe imprinted in his head.

A kiss in the garden as fireworks had exploded over their heads. Chloe's silky-soft curves beneath his hands. The raging hunger of his youthful hormones as she'd returned the favor with an innocence that had nearly brought him to his knees. He'd put a stop to that soon enough, because that would have been true insanity, but he'd touched her plenty, her short, cherry-colored dress an irresistible temptation, with even softer skin to be found beneath.

His throat went so dry he almost crawled across the bar and poured the drink himself. If he lived to be a hundred, he would never forget the sound of her cries in his ear as he'd brought her untutored body to the peak of pleasure. It had nearly unmanned him.

He threw some bills at the bartender as he arrived with his drink. Took a sustaining gulp of the Scotch, welcoming its smooth, hot burn.

"I didn't figure Puccini as your thing."

A smile touched his mouth as Santo, his youngest brother, slid into place beside him at the bar. Dressed in a sharp black tux, he had their mother's coloring, as light as he and Lazzero were dark. Electing to scruff up his impossibly perfect golden good looks tonight with some dangerous-looking stubble, it did nothing to make him look any less angelic.

"Not so much," Nico commented drily. The arts were Santo's thing. "Who's the lucky female? I'm assuming you brought one."

"Kathleen O'Keefe, a business reporter for one of the dailies." Santo caught the bartender's attention and ordered two glasses of wine before he leaned back against the bar, arms crossed over his pristine Armani. "We're sitting two boxes over from you. I tried to get your attention, but you were someplace else. Who's the hot blonde, by the way? She would have distracted me, too."

"Helene Schmidt, the president of Stil 049."

"Gorgeous and successful," Santo murmured. "Tell me this is ending up horizontal."

"I don't date clients."

Santo fixed him with an assessing look. "*Santo*

Nico," he drawled. "Mamma had the names all wrong."

Nico took a pull of his Scotch in response.

"I saw your little bird the other night," Santo said idly. "She looked...*fantastic*. When are you going to admit she is a problem for you, *fratello*? Or should we saint you now and get it over with?"

Nico swirled the amber liquid in his glass. "She isn't my *little bird*. And I took care of that problem a long time ago."

"You think so?" Amusement dripped from his brother's voice. "The first step in addressing a problem is admitting you have one. Chloe is all grown up, Nico. She doesn't need your brand of protection anymore."

She sure as hell did. She'd been as delicate as a wisp of wind in his office tonight. And what had he done? He'd piled more pressure on her.

"Anyway," Santo said with a dramatic sweep of his palm, "Kathleen gave me a piece of intel last night in bed. I wanted to pass it along."

"Save that for yourself," Nico deadpanned. "I've never had any complaints in that area."

Santo's mouth quirked. "Very funny. Kathleen is a *business* reporter. Her editor had lunch with

Giorgio Russo last week. Giorgio spent the whole lunch giving him the background scoop on the 'political unrest' at Evolution. He said he has half the board in his pocket."

Red blazed in his head. His hand tightening around the crystal tumbler he held, he absorbed a burn of pure fury. He'd been content to watch Giorgio spin his wheels with his fruitless internal campaign to discredit him, but taking it public was crossing the line. He wasn't worried about the board being solid behind him because he knew that they were. But if Giorgio was shooting his mouth off to journalists, it could *create* an aura of political instability around Evolution with the very forces that determined its future—the analysts, the market, the shareholders—worried the company would implode from the inside out. And that he couldn't have.

"Grazie," he murmured to Santo. "That is good information to have."

Santo lifted a brow. "What are you going to do?"

"Shut him down."

CHAPTER FOUR

THERE WERE PRIMA DONNAS and then there was Lashaunta. The pop singer took the concept to a whole other level.

Chloe buried her head in her hands as the diva walked off the set for the fifth time to take a phone call from her boyfriend, with whom she shared some strange kind of bizarre pseudo-addiction. From the high-end champagne she'd demanded for her dressing room to the red roses that needed to cover every surface because they put her in a good "mental place" to the incessant phone calls with Romeo, they hadn't captured even one decent piece of footage all day.

Given the singer went on tour for a month tomorrow, it was a problem. Chloe rubbed her palms against her temples, massaged the dull ache beginning to penetrate her skull. She must have been crazy to think she could do this. The timeline was insanely tight, with absolutely no room for miscues. If she went down in flames with this launch, so did Evolution.

You are only as good as your supporting team, Nico had counseled in their morning meetings in which she'd done her best to behave and listen. *Trust them to execute this for you.* Which she did. Now if only her pop sensation would save her torrid romance for the midnight hour so she could wrap this spot up before she and Nico left for Palm Beach on Friday. Which was key because Lashaunta kicked off the campaign in the middle of November, with Desdemona following her—a one-two punch that would hopefully put her perfumes on everyone's lips.

Lashaunta sauntered back onto the set. Chloe took a deep breath. Walked down onto the set and took the pop singer through the concept for Be. *Again*. Lashaunta stared at her blank-faced. *OMG*.

"Can you think of a moment in your life," Chloe said patiently, "when you realized you had become what you were destined to be? When you let yourself be stripped down, naked, *raw*, to hell with what anyone else thought, because this was *you*, and you couldn't be anything else but what you are?"

The pop singer's exotic eyes brightened. "Sure. When I met Donnie," she said dreamily. "I mean, we are *real* with each other."

Chloe almost cried. "I was hoping for something a little more impactful than that. Not that Donnie isn't that," she hastily backtracked when Lashaunta eyed her, "but you know what I mean."

The diva pressed red-tipped fingers to her wide, passionate mouth. *"Yes,"* she finally said. "When I was standing on the stage at the Billboard Awards last year. I'd just sung 'Butterfly.' It was the craziest moment—the applause went on forever. I just stood there and drank it all in. In wonder, really, because this was just me—the girl from a tiny Caribbean island no one's ever heard of. I knew then," she said huskily, "that finally I'd arrived. It was full-on, girl."

Chloe remembered it. It had held her and the rest of the world transfixed—the moment almost religious in its intensity. "Can you please," she said evenly, "say that on camera?"

"No problem."

Chloe was an hour late for her media training

session by the time she flew upstairs to her office. Her headache had, unfortunately, elected to go south, but at least Lashaunta's spot was in the can. Which faded to a pleasant memory as her media trainer, whom she liked to refer to as her military drill instructor, pushed her through two hours of brutal interviews. Which didn't go well because she hadn't had time to read the prep notes and was flying by the seat of her pants.

"Better," said the drill instructor when she'd finished her latest effort. "But can we do it again? I'm not really *feeling* the passion when it comes to what you do."

She gritted her teeth. Felt huge sympathy for Lashaunta. She knew what she was *feeling*, and it was an almost uncontrollable urge to strangle her instructor to a slow and painful death.

Head throbbing, she pulled off her mic. "No," she said, getting to her feet. "I'm done. We can pick this up tomorrow."

The trainer's mouth fell open. "We have two hours left. And you have your big interview on Friday."

"Then we'd better hope I improve by then."

She snatched up her lab coat and stormed out of

her office, the crew staring after her. And walked straight into a brick wall in Nico.

It hadn't been that bad, Chloe told herself a couple of hours later as she pulled herself out of the pool in the rooftop executive spa, a perk that put working at Evolution on top of every Manhattanite's dream job list.

Nico *had* been furious with her for ditching the media training session, but thankfully he'd been on his way into a meeting. And she *had* explained what her day had been like to her stony-faced boss.

And who cared, really? She grabbed a thick towel and blotted the water from her skin. She still had work to do in the lab after the break she'd decided was mandatory. She was doing her best, and if he didn't want to see that, well, *tough*.

A glass of cucumber water beckoned, along with the steam room to ease a few of the knots in her shoulders. Slinging the towel over her shoulder, she hummed a tune as she pushed open the glass doors to the luxurious cream marble space. The sight of Nico in low-slung graphite swim trunks lounging on a bench stopped her in her tracks.

She couldn't be this unlucky. Her pulse bounded beneath her skin as she took him in. She definitely wasn't staying—that was for sure. But first, she needed to stop drooling over the jaw-dropping washboard abs, which seemed as if they might be a gift from heaven as the sweat poured down them. The muscles that bunched thick in his shoulders. The *thighs* that were so powerful they took her thoughts to places they most definitely shouldn't go.

He was dead to her. He had smashed her heart into little pieces and left her like roadkill by the side of the highway. She kept that thought top of mind as she lifted her gaze to his. Not his normal calm, steely gray, she registered, noting the heated flame that burned there.

A thread of unease tightened around her chest, then unraveled so fast her heart began to whirl. So he hadn't cooled off.

"Enjoy," she murmured, pivoting on her heel. "I've changed my mind. I think I'll shower instead."

He set an even gaze on hers. "Sit down, Chloe.

I think we can share the same space without taking each other apart."

She wasn't actually so sure that was true.

Nico could have cursed Santo. Because all he could think of beyond his extreme aggravation with the woman opposite him was how amazing she looked in that swimsuit.

You couldn't even say it was provocative. There was too much material to the fuchsia-colored bikini for that. Which made it all the more enticing because it left so much of her slim, curvaceous figure unexposed.

Where she'd been all long, slim limbs at eighteen, she had filled out in all the right places since. *Not a teenager anymore.* A beautiful, desirable woman he was sure some man had already discovered. *If* he'd been able to get past her mile-high walls. Why he hated that idea was frankly irrational.

Irritated at his own weakness, he swept a towel across his face. Focused his anger on her instead as she wrapped a towel sarong-style around herself and sat opposite him on the marble bench.

"You cost the company a thousand dollars

today. You can't just decide you've had enough and walk out. We made a deal, one you are going to stick to, or I swear I'll pull the plug on your campaign."

She lifted her chin, eyes shimmering, dark pools of light. "I'm only one person, Nico. I'm spreading myself too thin. Something's got to give."

"Stop micromanaging your team, then, and let them do their job."

"We wouldn't have gotten Lashaunta's spot filmed today without me." She shifted on the bench, drawing his eye to a creamy stretch of undeniably luscious thigh.

"I'm terrible at the media stuff," she announced flatly. "I told you I would be. What's the point?"

He tore his gaze away from those delectable thighs. "You would be better at it if you knew your key messages. Have you even looked at them?"

She stared at him, affronted. "Have they been giving you *reports* on me?"

"I asked for one."

Hot color shaded her cheeks. "I fell asleep reading them last night."

"Because you were in the lab until ten o'clock." He shook his head. "You are *banned* from the lab until you master this, Chloe. Not one step past that door."

A slight widening of her big brown eyes was her only reaction. She leaned her head back against the tile and eyed him. "John Chisolm told me this morning my father took a step back last year. That, in essence, you have been running Evolution ever since. What was he talking about?"

Nico kept his face bland. "Your father decided it was time to enjoy life a bit more. He had me, so he could afford to do so."

"My father didn't know the meaning of downtime," Chloe countered. "Evolution was his passion. He always said he'd run it until either his mind or his body gave out."

Dannazione. He hated this. "Later life tends to give you perspective," he murmured.

Her gaze sharpened on him. "What is it you aren't telling me?"

"You're reading too much into it," he said flatly. He wiped another rivulet of sweat from his eyes. "What you *might* expend your energy on is convincing your uncle to put a muzzle on himself. All his smear campaign is doing is making him look like a fool while everyone who plays a role in the future of this company worries the internal politics will make us implode."

She was silent for a long moment. "Give me a reason to trust you," she said quietly. "Because right now I feel like I am missing a piece of the puzzle and I don't know what it is. If my father had you running the company, why didn't he tell Giorgio that? Why not make it clear what the succession plan was? Why let it fester like this?"

The thought that he should just *tell* her flashed through his head. Because what did it matter now? Martino was dead. Was keeping Chloe in the dark doing more harm than good? Except, he acknowledged, he'd given Martino his word not to say anything, and his word was his word. As for Giorgio? He'd soon hang himself on his own insurrection.

He set his gaze on Chloe's. "You know you can trust me. Have I ever broken a promise to you?"

"Yes," she whipped back, fire in her eyes. "The one where you promised *to be there* for me and then you weren't."

* * *

Oh, hell. Chloe bumped her head against the wall as if to knock some sense into herself. She'd sworn she wasn't going there. Had *promised* herself she wasn't going there. And then she had.

Nico closed his eyes. Exhaled. "I have *always* been there for you," he said finally, opening them again. "I started something I shouldn't have that summer with you, Chloe. I was your father's protégé, four years older than you, a *lifetime* at that age. We both knew it wasn't going to end well. It was far too...*complicated* and you were far too vulnerable. You were looking for something I couldn't give."

She blinked. Attempted to take in everything he'd just said. Everything she'd never been privy to because he'd never explained it to her.

"I—I never asked you for anything," she stammered. "I was eighteen, Nico. I just thought we had something good."

"You were infatuated with me," he said matter-of-factly. "For me it was hormones. I wanted you, but I didn't want the entanglements that came with it. You wanted everything—the moonlight, the candles, the romance. I couldn't give you that.

Better you go off and find a nice French boy-friend who could."

Instead, he'd kissed her to within an inch of her life, branded her with his touch as he'd made her come apart in his arms and then walked away, leaving that comparison to haunt her every time she'd kissed a man since. Because kissing Nico, experiencing the passion she had felt in his arms, had felt like a revelation.

Her stomach twisted into a tight, hot knot. "So," she said, eyes on his, "you slept with Angelique—why? Because you simply moved on?"

"Because I thought it was the easiest way to drive home the point we were done." He rubbed a palm against the stubble on his jaw. "Perhaps it wasn't the right way to handle it, but I'm not sure anything else would have worked."

Because she'd pursued him afterward. Refused to take no for an answer.

Humiliation flared through her, hot and deep. "You could have just explained it to me, Nico. I would have *gotten it*, I assure you. Because honestly," she said with a shoulder shrug, pride driving her on, "I was simply looking to sample what you offer so freely to other women. That legendary *expertise* you're known for. It would have been an excellent base to work from."

"You think so?" The low rumble in his voice should have been her first clue she'd crossed a line. Some invisible marker that tumbled them straight from a safe, combative place into entirely unknown territory. The incendiary glimmer in his eyes, glowing like the last banked embers of a fire, cemented it. "I think you have no idea what happens when you play with fire. Someone always gets burned, I can assure you. Which is why I walked away ten years ago. Because *this* is never happening between us."

Her heart felt as if it had fallen into a deep, dark pit with no bottom. Swallowing hard, she searched for air. Half of her wanted to know what it was like to walk into the fire—to *get* burned, because she'd never felt as alive as she'd felt in his arms that night. The other half wanted to run for safety—to retreat into the sheltered, familiar world she had always existed in.

She felt shaky, unsure of everything in that moment. *Nothing* felt concrete anymore. Everything seemed to be mired in a gray haze she had no idea how to navigate.

Not messing up this chance to prove herself Nico had given her seemed to be the only coherent thought she had.

"Maybe your lesson in all this," she said, fixing her gaze on his, "is that you don't need to make decisions for me, Nico. I'm perfectly capable of making them myself. In fact," she said quietly, "I wish I had."

She left then. Because it seemed the only rational thing to do.

CHAPTER FIVE

WHY HAD SHE agreed to this?

Chloe paced her office twenty-four hours after her confrontation with Nico, the key messages she'd been attempting to inhale for her big interview circling her head like puzzle pieces that refused to form themselves into a coherent picture.

The interview was tomorrow morning, looming like her worst nightmare. *D-day.* She *knew* how important it was. The feature piece for the fashion section of the most distinguished paper in the nation was an amazing opportunity to gain profile for Evolution at a time when the company desperately needed it. But if one more person attempted to imprint that fact into her head, she was going to scream.

She collapsed on her mother's Louis XVI sofa and took a deep breath. She was being ridiculous. Of course she could do this. She just needed to get over the block in her head. She thought it might have something to do with the million things she *wasn't* doing at the moment that needed to be done.

Another thing she didn't *need* appeared in the doorway of her office. Dressed in a dark gray suit, a lilac shirt and an eggplant tie that enhanced his swarthy coloring, Nico looked disgustingly energized at seven o'clock in the evening. As if he could take on another full day with one hand tied behind his back. A bit *dazzling*.

She cursed her ever-present awareness of him. She'd been doing so well keeping their relationship on a business footing, but that confrontation in the spa had ignited something between them she couldn't seem to turn off.

"I'm studying," she grumbled, waving the papers in front of her at him. "No need to lecture."

"You look exhausted," he said bluntly. "I heard the session today didn't go great."

"Nope. No surprises there." She sat back against the sofa and exhaled a long sigh. "I have no idea why I'm so blocked. I can't seem to articulate myself the way I want to."

He crossed his arms over his chest. "Then we'll work through it together."

She sat up straight. Eyed him warily. Nico and his overbearing tactics were the *last* thing she needed right now.

"I can handle this myself."

"You could," he conceded. "But I can help. I've done a million of these interviews."

With effortless, supreme confidence, she assumed, watching helplessly as he shrugged off his jacket, slung it over the back of a chair and walked to the bar, where he pulled a bottle of wine from the rack and set out two glasses.

"*That* is not going to help."

He ignored her and opened the wine. "You need to relax. You're so far in your head right now you can't see the forest from the trees."

Likely true. Although she wished she could attain some kind of clarity when it came to *him*. Figure out what he was keeping from her. She'd talked to Mireille about their father's supposed step back. It might have been true, Mireille had conceded, that their father had taken a bit of a foot off the gas over the past year, but he had been sixty-two. Would it really have been so unexpected for him to want to take a break?

No, but why, then, wouldn't he have simply

communicated that to Giorgio? She'd spoken to her uncle, who'd insisted his version of events was true. When she'd voiced her apprehension his campaign to discredit Nico would destabilize Evolution, it had been like talking to a brick wall. Which did worry her. She had no idea what he was up to—and that couldn't be good.

Another issue she couldn't tackle right *now*. Nico carried the wine and glasses over to the sofa and sat down beside her. All of a sudden, the delicate piece of furniture seemed so much smaller with him in it. Long legs sprawled in front of him, wineglass in hand, his shirtsleeves rolled up to reveal corded, muscular forearms, he was impossible to ignore.

She'd tried to convince herself that Gerald, the handsome Frenchman she'd dated for a few months, had been just as attractive. But that had been wishful thinking. Nico had a hint of the street in him beneath that outward elegance he'd cultivated. The *rough set of cards life had dealt him*, according to her father. It made him intimidating, fascinating, *dangerous* in a way Gerald could never hope to emulate.

He eyed her. "So what exactly," he asked, pointing his wineglass at her, "is it that you are struggling with?"

"The big-picture questions. My creative vision… I have no idea how to explain it." She waved a hand at him. "Everyone thinks it's this mystical thing that involves divine inspiration, when in reality, it's like a puzzle I have to solve. A painting I need to layer bit by bit. It's different for each individual scent I develop depending on whom I'm creating it for."

He considered that for a moment. "Maybe you need to use some of your mother's techniques."

"Like what?"

"She would use the interviewer as an example, for instance. Pretend she was creating a scent for him or her. It was a brilliant technique—got the journalist very involved in the process. They were fascinated by it."

"Which is fine if you can think on the spot like my mother could." Chloe pursed her lips. "It takes me months, *years*, to come up with a fragrance."

"But you must have some sense when you meet someone what will suit them. What do you do when you design custom fragrances?"

She thought about it for a moment. "I do an interview of sorts, a history taking if you like, to get a sense of who the person is. Their past, present, what they like, dislike. It would give me an initial idea of what kinds of scents they would prefer, but it wouldn't direct me, if you know what I mean. Someone can say to me they like beachy, breezy fragrances, but that might not be what suits them at all. Or what they're really asking for."

He took a sip of his wine. Swirled the ruby-red liquid in his glass. "Try it with me, then. You've never designed a fragrance for me. I would be the perfect test case."

She gave him a wary look. "Right now?"

"Why not?" His eyes held the spark of a challenge. "It would be the perfect test run. I know you can do this, Chloe. Stop censoring yourself and let your instincts take over."

She thought censoring herself was exactly what she should be doing when it came to him. But she had never been one to back down from a challenge.

"Fine," she agreed. "But I need a prop."

* * *

Nico eyed Chloe as she sat down on the sofa with a testing tray in her hands. He was capable of keeping his hands off her, that he knew, but *her* putting her hands on him? That might be a different story. That had been where all their issues had begun in the first place.

He lifted a brow. "Are you planning on putting those on me?"

"No." She observed the skeptical note in his voice. "That would be counterproductive. Everything would blend into one another. I'll put them on scent strips and have you give your impression. It won't be the full test I'd do if I was creating a perfume for someone, but it will give you an idea of the process."

"Bene." He settled back against the sofa, wineglass in hand. She plucked the glass from his fingers and set it on the table.

"The red wine will throw your sense of smell off."

"Right." He studied the focus on her intent, serious face. Found it more than a bit sexy. "Do we start with the interview, then?"

"I'm going to skip it because I know you. We'll

start with the scent test instead. I can fill the rest in myself."

He opened his hands wide. "I'm all yours."

A flush stained her olive cheeks at the unintended innuendo. He stared at it, fascinated. When was the last time he'd seen a woman do *that*? Chloe had an innocence, a transparency about her that had always amazed him—as if she had been poured straight from the source, uncontaminated by life. Which, he conceded, was pretty much the case.

Was that what had always drawn him to her? Because it was exotic to him, *compelling*? Because it seemed to rub off on everyone who came into contact with her, reminding them of an innocence, a *goodness*, that still existed in the world? Or was it just because he'd always wanted what he couldn't have?

She dabbed two feather-shaped scent strips with a unique essence from the glass bottles. "Think of it as a blind taste test," she instructed, handing them to him. "Except you're smelling instead. This is you picking your favorite scents in a process of elimination that will help me choose the top, middle and base notes of the fragrance."

"So you're not going to tell me what they are?"

"No. Take one in either hand," she directed. "When you smell the one on your left, it's going to be clean and woodsy, with a hint of warmth to it. When you switch to the other, you will smell something deeper, less clean. Tobacco and spice dominate. Now you come back to the initial scent, it's crisp and clean, airy, not as warm as it was before. Then you go back to the second. There's tobacco and spice, a boldness, a complexity to it. A *sensuality*."

He brought the first scent strip to his nose, fascinated to find the experience exactly as she had described—the first light and less complex, the second rich and seductive.

"Close your eyes," Chloe encouraged. "Give yourself over to it. Let yourself be hedonistic, fully aware of your senses. Scent is *intimate*," she murmured. "Intensely personal. React to it. Let *it* tell you where you want to go."

Nico closed his eyes. Listened to her talk him through each pair. Found himself utterly distracted by the passion with which she approached her calling. How sensual an experience it actually was.

On they went, bouncing back and forth. Him choosing his favorite and giving his gut reaction, Chloe making notes.

The slide of her fingertips against his, the sensual lilt to her voice, the accidental brush of the soft curve of her breast against his arm were the most potent aphrodisiacs he'd ever encountered. It turned him hard as stone.

Not his brightest idea.

"And these two?" she prompted.

"The one on the left," he murmured, "reminds me of the cottage we used to go to in Maine as kids. The ocean."

She nodded. "That's called a scent imprint. A memory associated with a scent. We all have them. They're very specific to us personally. Good. And the other?"

"Warmer. Intense, illusive. It smells like—" *Her.* Like the fragrance she'd always worn. Except on Chloe it was exotic and intoxicating, the way it came off the heat of her skin. "Summer," he finished lamely.

She handed him two more strips. "And these?"

"Tropical," he said of the first one. "Sweet. Rich."

"And the next?"

He inhaled. Found himself in the middle of a smoky, earthy scent that was just a little...*dirty.*

"Sex." He opened his eyes and fixed them on hers. "That one is definitely sex."

Her eyes widened. Shimmered with a heat that snagged his insides. Potent and thick, the air around them suddenly seemed dense—layers deep—all his good intentions evaporating as her gaze dropped to his mouth. Stayed there.

She drifted closer, her floral scent melding with his, the hitched sound of her breathing stirring his senses. It took every ounce of his willpower not to close the last few centimeters between them and cover those lush lips with his, because a decade later, he still remembered how sweet they were...how perfect she'd tasted beneath him. How *forbidden.*

"Chloe," he murmured. "Are we almost done? I feel like we should be done now."

"Yes," she breathed, dragging her gaze back up to his. "You're very good, by the way. That one has lots of indole in it. It comes from—" She sank her teeth into her full bottom lip. "Well... you know."

He didn't know. Didn't *want* to know. Because the only place his mind wanted to go right now started with an *s* and ended with an *x*. And that couldn't happen with this particular woman. Not now. Not ever.

Chloe cleared her throat, her eyes dark, liquid, so brown they were almost black. "There's two more. But we could probably leave those because I'm sure I know which way I'm going to go."

"Good. Let's do that." He reached for his wine and took a gulp. Ruthlessly pulled his libido back under control.

"So," he prompted, "what is your analysis?"

Chloe wasn't sure how her brain was supposed to function after that look Nico had just given her. As if he wanted to consume her whole. As if *she* was what he wanted to get intimate with. Because that hadn't been her imagination talking, she was sure of it.

Her head spun as she made a show of gathering up her materials and stowing them on the tray. Knowing after all this time the attraction between them wasn't one-sided like she'd thought it had been, that it was clear and *present*, was a bit mind-boggling. Also head-scratching was the fact that for a moment there, she'd felt compelled to play with that fire he'd declared off bounds. Which *was* crazy. For so many reasons.

She closed trembling fingers around the stem of her wineglass, lifted it to her mouth and took a sip. Gathered her brain back into some sort of working order because she wasn't done yet.

"You wear my mother's Voluttuoso," she began, setting her gaze on his, "which is a gorgeous fragrance, one of my favorites. And it does reflect the innate...*sensuality* about you. But I would have gone with something different."

"I like that fragrance," he countered. "I think it suits me. Why not it?"

"Because you're more complex than that," she said quietly. "Vetiver, the warm Indian grass that predominates in Voluttuoso, is sexy, but you have a strength, a *toughness* about you that comes from your past. With Voluttuoso, it's only showing one facet of you. If it were me, I would veer toward something darker and more complex."

"Such as?"

"Something with a base note of the tobacco you were drawn to, for instance. I'd have predicted that. It has depth, like you. Some cedar," she continued thoughtfully, "to reinforce the tobacco and to bring in that scent memory you have of your early years at the cottage. Some other warm notes to give it added complexity," she continued, formulas shifting in her head like puzzle pieces. "Amber or nutmeg, perhaps. And jasmine, definitely jasmine, for that sensual edge."

A smile curved her mouth. "Bold, rich and *haunting*."

He lifted a brow. "Haunting?"

She gave a self-conscious shrug. "A turn of phrase. Evocative words sell perfumes."

"And so do you," he murmured. "I was buying everything you were selling, Chloe. Hook, line and sinker. You had me on the edge of my seat." He pointed his wineglass at her. "You didn't *tell* me about the creative process, you *demonstrated* it. Do that tomorrow and you'll be gold."

Or she could blow it completely and let everyone down.

CHAPTER SIX

ARMED WITH A strong cup of coffee and as much confidence as she could muster, Chloe played host to the hip, young journalist Carrie Mayer from the nation's most respected daily newspaper at 10:00 a.m. the next morning in her office. The reporter spent the first few minutes raving about the decor, which only reminded Chloe of what a big personality her mother had been and cranked up her nerves yet another notch.

How could she possibly *be* that?

But she refused to retreat back into her head, because this was too important. Luckily, she and Carrie clicked and were soon whizzing through the questions. Chloe wasn't perfect in her answers, knew she'd missed some of her key messages along the way she'd probably get her hand slapped for, but she kept things on track, even when Carrie asked about her mother's death and what she had meant to her.

It was, however, when she went through the scent test with Carrie and offered her personal recommendation that the journalist's eyes lit up. "Brilliant," she murmured, madly scribbling notes. "Can I quote all of that, or are there trade secrets in there I can't use?"

Chloe told her to go ahead and use it. Gave the reporter a bottle of her mother's Cygne Blanc, which would suit her perfectly.

Nico, Chloe admitted as she showed Carrie out, was very smart. She might just tell him that. But first, she had a whirlwind shopping trip with Mireille to accomplish in the lunch hour before her and Nico's flight to Palm Beach, because she had absolutely nothing to wear that was in any way suitable for the black-tie charity fund-raiser that evening that attracted the world's elite.

Luckily, Mireille was miraculous with clothes and knew just where to shop. In the space of an hour, they'd found the perfect gown for the Champagne and Diamonds fund-raiser. They'd also acquired a couple of outfits for the warmer Palm Beach weather while they were at it, given Chloe and Nico would spend the weekend at the Di Fiore brothers' luxurious South Beach estate.

Nico had made golf plans with clients tomorrow, which gave Chloe a chance to enjoy a day in the sun. Which was, she acknowledged, another source of nerves. Keeping her attraction to Nico under wraps from a distance was one thing—doing it while they shared the same roof was another.

It was not helpful, then, when she met Nico at the small private airport in New Jersey they would fly out of, to find him dressed in black jeans and a long-sleeved crew-necked sweater in dove gray that matched his eyes. Draped against an unused check-in desk while he tapped away on his phone, he was so stunning every woman in the tiny lounge was making him the preboarding entertainment.

He gave a pointed look at his watch. "We're up next."

"I had to shop. My slave driver of a boss has me toiling all hours."

A curve of his amazing mouth. "How did the interview go?"

"Well, I think. You were right," she conceded with a tip of her head, "the reporter loved the essence test. She said it was brilliant content for the piece." She shrugged a shoulder. "I'm not sure I got every key message across. I was too nervous with the difficult questions. But I did okay."

His smile deepened into one of those rare lazy ones he offered so infrequently, it made her breath catch in her chest. "Then I'm sure it will be great. Now you can relax and enjoy the weekend."

"Yes." She swallowed past the fluttering feeling inside her. "Thank you," she said quietly. "For helping me. You were right. I was so far inside my head, I couldn't seem to get out."

His gray eyes warmed. "I promised you I would be there for you, Chloe, and I will. You are not in this alone."

And why did she feel so reassured by that? She pondered the answer as an official gave them a nod and they were escorted across the tarmac to the sleek ten-person Evolution jet, where the pilot was ready to go. Why was her guard beginning to come down with Nico?

Because she was starting to wonder if she'd been wrong about him, in more than one way? Because everyone she spoke to at Evolution loved working for him—*appreciated* his leadership?

Because he *had* been there for her—exactly as

he'd promised? Or had it been that moment in her office where she'd become shockingly aware that the chemistry between her and Nico wasn't one-sided? Was that messing with her head?

She had no idea *what to do* with that particular piece of information. Knew it wasn't wise to pursue it—that Nico had been right about that—but she couldn't seem to get it out of her head.

She was so exhausted, she slept most of the short flight to Miami. Which was helpful, because by the time they arrived and stepped onto the waiting helicopter that would take them to the Di Fiores' South Beach estate, she'd gotten her second wind.

The ultra-modern villa the Di Fiore brothers had built on the ocean was all sleek, square lines, with a spectacular view from its streamlined, wide-open spaces. She felt herself exhaling, the tension seeping out of her bones, as she breathed in the humid, fragrant, warm air.

Boasting double-height ceilings that led to an oversize infinity-edge pool, a custom Italian kitchen and a hand-carved mahogany wine cellar that made her head spin with its extravagant selection, it was Chloe's idea of heaven. Lazzero, who spent the most time at the house, enjoying the party scene for business purposes, had hired a lovely housekeeper, who showed Chloe to a gorgeous, airy bedroom on the second floor, done in dark woods and stark white, with colorful accents thrown in.

Chloe fell in love with the stunning pink-and-orange bougainvillea that seemed to climb into her ethereal bedroom and wished dearly she could take a dip in the ocean before dinner, but since they were due for sunset cocktails at the Buchanans' nearby estate, it would have to wait.

Energized by the heady aroma of tropical flowers and the salty, fresh sea air, Chloe slipped on the gorgeous coffee-colored lace dress she'd bought with Mireille at lunch. Floor length and glamorous, with pretty cap sleeves and a deep plunging back, it was a daring style she never would have chosen on her own.

Catching her hair up in a loose knot, she spritzed on her favorite perfume and declared herself done.

Nico was leaning against the railing, staring at a view of forever, when Chloe joined him on the terrace that overlooked the ocean. A waft of her unmistakable intoxicating perfume hit him just before she did. Then it was his heart going *ka-boom* as he turned around and took in the sight of her dressed in a lacy sophisticated number that echoed the creamy color of the silky expanse of skin it revealed.

If he hadn't been fully in lust by the time he'd covered off the delectable curves, he was when he took in her sexy disheveled hairstyle, which left her silky dark curls half up and half down. There was only one thing a man wanted to do when a woman wore her hair like that, and that was to dismantle it completely.

If she was his. Which she wasn't.

He swallowed hard. Santo might be right. He might have a problem. He'd been so far under Chloe's spell during that perfume-testing routine, he'd fled the room moments after it had mercifully ended. Sharing a villa with her wasn't necessarily a great choice either, but with his place ten minutes away from the Buchanans', it would have been silly not to take advantage of it.

What had Santo said? Admitting you had a problem was the first step toward solving it?

Chloe flashed him an uncertain look from beneath those long, amazing lashes of hers. "Am I not dressed appropriately? Mireille thought this would be perfect for tonight. But maybe it's too much?"

"You look gorgeous," he said quietly. "We should go so we aren't late."

She tipped her head back, luminous brown eyes resting on his. "Are you okay? You seem off."

"I'm good." He placed a hand at the small of her back to direct her toward the stairs, his palm nearly spanning her delicate spine. The satiny softness of her skin beneath his fingers unfurled a curl of heat inside him, one he ruthlessly leashed. He might have a problem, but he knew how to deal with it.

They made the quick, ten-minute drive through Palm Beach's quiet, exclusive streets, behind whose twelve-foot hedges had once resided some of America's oldest families—the Kennedys, Du Ponts, Posts and Fords had all had homes there. The Buchanans' ornate Palm Beach mansion, however, was the king of them all. An eclectic mix of many of the great European architectures—Venetian, Spanish, Portuguese and

Moorish—it sat directly on the ocean, more a palace than a mansion, rising majestically among fifteen acres of manicured, glorious gardens.

The statement property mirrored the big personality of its billionaire owners, Josh and Evelyn Buchanan. Josh, a big, bombastic Brit who'd been a close friend of Martino Russo's, had made his money in electronics and now owned an English football team. He'd fallen in love with his American wife, Evelyn, three decades ago and chosen to stay, building Palacio en el Mar, the "Palace on the Sea," for her.

Josh and Evelyn greeted them warmly, introducing them around the poolside soiree where the crème de la crème of the world's elite were gathered to hear the legendary pop star Rodrigo Carrera in a private concert.

It was a magnificent setting—the sun a ball of fire as it sank into the Atlantic, the lazy jazz band that preceded Carrera excellent, the affluent crowd, decked out in their diamonds and black-tie apparel, supremely elegant.

A glass of champagne in his hand, Nico focused on the valuable networking opportunities, rather than the beautiful woman at his side, ensured he and Chloe made that public, political statement of unanimity so necessary for Evolution's stability right now, which was recorded for posterity's sake by the society photographers in attendance.

Chloe tried hard to exercise the same enviable networking skills Nico possessed throughout the cocktail hour and dinner. She found it wasn't so awful as she'd imagined, easier than it had once been for her to complete the endless rounds of socializing with the budding confidence she'd developed and Vivre to talk about.

But it didn't come naturally to her—the ability to make casual small talk, to forge connections out of a throwaway comment someone made. She found herself more susceptible than usual, as a result, to the attentions of the Buchanans' handsome son, Oliver, whose attention over dinner had drawn her out of herself.

Tall and blond, with the most piercing blue eyes she'd ever seen, he was gorgeous. Successful. *Nice.* Exactly the kind of man a woman with a healthy sense of self-preservation should gravitate toward. Unfortunately, that didn't seem to be her. Never had been.

She accepted his offer of another glass of champagne as dinner broke up and the guests mingled on the terrace, waiting for Carrera to begin. Watched as Nico laughed at something the beautiful redhead he'd been sitting next to at dinner had said.

Tall and statuesque, with the perfect bone structure of a runway model, she was stunning. Everything Chloe wasn't. He wasn't looking at *her* as if she had a garbage sack on as he had Chloe earlier. He was looking at her as if she was utterly his type. It hurt in a way she couldn't even begin to articulate. Didn't want to articulate.

Her skin stung, her heart felt sore in her chest. Why had it always been Nico? Why couldn't she just move on? Would it have been different, she wondered, if he'd broken her heart like he surely would have done those years ago? Would she have had closure when it came to him? Because every man since had been a poor substitute— Nico the benchmark by which she had judged them all.

If they could make her feel her emotions right

to the pit of her stomach…if they could make her heart race as he did.

Nico looked up from his conversation with the redhead. Slid his gaze over her. Over the proprietary hand Oliver had placed at her waist. For a single, heart-stopping moment, a flash of heat blazed in his gray gaze. It scorched through her. Singed her right to her toes.

He wanted her, but he didn't want to want her. The very visible slip in his daunting self-control rocked her back on her heels. Stole her breath. Then the redhead said something to Nico and he turned away.

Chloe stood there, heart beating a jagged edge. Oliver bent his head to hers. "Let's dance," he murmured. "Carrera is coming on now."

She forced a smile and followed him to the dance floor. She had promised herself she was going to relax and enjoy herself this weekend. Pining after Nico, thinking thoughts that were inherently *unwise* when it came to him, was not accomplishing that. If she were smart, she'd do exactly what Nico was doing—pretend this thing between them didn't exist.

By the time midnight rolled around, however,

and Carrera was done with his intimate, fabulous concert, his voice as rich and amazing as it had been in his heyday, Chloe was officially done. She was sure she didn't have one more word of small talk left in her.

"Ready to go?" she asked Nico hopefully.

He nodded. "Let's find Josh and Evelyn and say good-night."

They wound their way through the thick crowd toward their hosts. A feminine voice, with a Southern drawl, cut through the din.

"Nico."

Chloe turned to see a beautiful blonde approaching them. Elegant and undeniably striking with her sparkling blue eyes and chic, sleek bob that angled fashionably to her ear, she moved with a grace and fluidity that captured the eye.

Chloe looked up at Nico, wondering who she was. Found his face frozen solid, not one whisper of emotion visible.

A former lover? She quickly discarded the idea as the woman drew upon them. She had to be in her midfifties. As gorgeous up close as she had been from afar, she must have been outrageously beautiful when she was younger. She still was.

The woman stopped in front of them, her gaze trained on Nico. Nico said nothing, an oddity with his impeccable manners. The woman ignored Chloe completely, waving a fluttering, nervous hand at Nico. "Evelyn just told me you were here. I had no idea. We— I arrived late."

Nico's expression hardened. "I hope you caught some of the concert. It was excellent." He nodded toward Josh and Evelyn, who were seeing guests off. "If you'll excuse us, we were on our way out."

The woman flinched. Chloe drew in a breath. Who was she? And why was Nico being so rude to her?

The blonde shifted her attention to Chloe, as if seeking assistance. "I'm sorry." She held out a perfectly manicured hand. "I'm Joelle Davis. Formerly Di Fiore. Nico's—"

"—mother," Nico finished. "In the biological sense, anyway."

Chloe's stomach dropped. *His mother?* All she'd ever known about Joelle Di Fiore was that she and Nico's father had divorced before his death and Nico never, ever talked about her.

"A pleasure," she murmured, taking Joelle's hand, because it seemed impolite not to.

"As I said," Nico repeated curtly, setting a hand on Chloe's waist, "we were on our way out. You'll have to excuse us."

"Nico." There was no mistaking the appeal in his mother's voice, the raw edge that slid across Chloe's skin. "I hate the way we left things in New York. I don't want it to be this way." She shook her head and fixed her too-bright gaze on her son. "I've recognized my mistake. Can't you at least acknowledge that?"

"Bene," he agreed, his voice utterly devoid of emotion. *Fine.* "I recognize you recognize you made a mistake. Can we go now?"

Chloe gasped. Joelle's blue eyes glistened. "Nico—"

A tall, distinguished silver-haired man separated himself from the crowd and headed toward them. A stony look claimed Nico's face. He pressed his palm to Chloe's back. "If you'll excuse us."

They left Joelle Davis standing in the crowd. Said good-night to the Buchanans. Nico didn't say a word on the drive home, his face so closed

Chloe didn't dare open her mouth. She could feel the tension in him, coiled tight in his big body as he drove, his knuckles white as they clenched the steering wheel. It made her insides twist into a cold, hard knot.

When they arrived at the house, Nico threw his car keys on the entrance table and wished her a good night.

Chloe eyed him. "Do you want to talk about it?"

"No." He flicked her a glance. "Go to bed, Chloe. You look exhausted."

But she couldn't sleep. Her beautiful bedroom with its elegant four-poster bed was heavenly, the book she'd brought with her entertaining, but as exhausted as she was, she was too wired to settle.

She was worried about Nico. About the emotion he always held inside, her head spinning with curiosity about what had happened with his mother to evoke that kind of a reaction. Eventually, she slipped out of bed, put on her new white bikini and a cover-up dress and went downstairs. The house was in darkness, as was Nico's office as she padded across the hardwood floors, but the pool area was lit with recessed lighting, tranquil and inviting under a clear, starry night.

Nico must have gone to bed, she surmised, when she found the terrace deserted, too. It was still warm out, the air just the slightest bit cool on her skin as she took off her dress. A slight shiver moved through her as she descended the steps to the infinity pool with its magnificent view of the ocean. Still warm from the sun, the water was divine.

The heady fragrance of a dozen tropical flowers scenting the air, ideas for a new perfume filled her head. She swam twenty lazy laps with only a cavalcade of stars as her witness. When she had tired herself out, her limbs heavy, body rejuvenated, she climbed out of the pool and reached for a towel on the rack. Stopped dead in her tracks at the sight of Nico sprawled in a lounge chair.

Obscured by the shadows cast by the half wall that divided the pool and lounge area, a glass of what she assumed was whiskey dangling from his fingers, he looked disheveled in a way she'd never seen him before. His jacket and tie gone, the top few buttons of his shirt undone, his hair spiky and ruffled, he looked like he'd been there for a while.

Her gaze shifted to the whiskey bottle beside the chair, a good dent taken out of it. Back up to his stormy gray gaze. He raked it down over her still-dripping body in the brief white bikini, a frank, appraising look so raw and uncensored, it rocked her back on her heels.

Heat, wild heat, unraveled beneath her skin. Stained her cheeks. She'd always wondered what Nico unleashed looked like. *If* he ever unleashed himself. Now she knew.

She wrapped the towel around herself, tucking it against her chest with trembling fingers. "I didn't see you there."

"I figured." Low, intense, his voice was sandpaper rough. "You couldn't sleep?"

"No."

"I'm sure you will now."

She ignored the unsubtle dismissal and walked over to him on legs that felt like jelly, whether from the swim or the intensity of his stare, she wasn't quite sure. Up close, she could read the lust in his eyes, a stomach-curling need that shimmered through her insides. But there was also darker, angrier emotion. A combustibility, a *volatility* that burned there.

"You're angry with her," she said quietly.

He pointed a finger at her. "*Bingo.* You win the prize."

She swallowed hard. "You need to talk about it, Nico. It's not healthy to hold everything inside." When he simply continued to stare at her as if she hadn't even spoken, she sighed and pushed a stray hair out of her face. "We used to talk. We used to be...*friends.*"

His mouth twisted. "Can we just get one thing straight? We are not *friends*, Chloe. We were never friends."

She sank her teeth into her lip, the salty tang of blood staining her mouth. "What were we, then?"

He took a contemplative sip of his whiskey. "I don't think," he said decisively, "that should be a point of discussion tonight."

"Fine," she said calmly, more off balance by this barely censored version of Nico than she cared to admit. She sat down on the lounge chair next to him. "How about we talk about what happened tonight, then?"

He lifted a shoulder. "What's there to talk about?"

"The fact that your mother desperately wants a relationship with you and you threw it in her face."

His eyes flashed. "You have no idea what you're talking about."

"Then tell me. This is clearly eating you up inside."

He rested his head back against the chair. Stared at her with those incendiary gray eyes. "She walked out on us when I was fifteen."

Chloe's stomach contracted. Such a tough age to lose a mother. "Why did she leave?"

An entirely unhumorous smile stretched his mouth. "Do you have all night?"

"Yes." She curled up on the chair and tucked her legs beneath her. He gave her a long look, then turned his head to stare out at the ocean. She thought he would shut her down then, but he started talking instead.

"My mother met my father when he was a young stockbroker on Wall Street. She was a dance instructor from Brooklyn. She'd moved to New York from California to make it on Broadway. Then she got pregnant with me. She was bitter about it, had no interest in being a mother, but my father convinced her to have me. He desperately wanted kids. He started making a lot of money, and then she didn't care so much because she loved to spend it."

"My father was best man at their wedding, wasn't he?" Chloe asked, remembering the photos her father had shown her.

Nico nodded. "Those were the good years. Lazzero and Santo came along. We got a big house, had the fancy cars, everything that came with the Wall Street lifestyle. Then Martino decided to leave and start Evolution. My father thought about it, decided he was wasting his talent on his firm and left to start his own company."

"A stock brokerage?"

"No. One of his clients, a brilliant engineer, had developed a technology to block the effects of wireless fields when cell phones became popular—a tiny chip you could put on the back of your phone. It was revolutionary, had limitless potential, but the client didn't have the money to bring it to market on his own. My father went into business with him—sank every dollar he had into it."

Chloe was completely intrigued. "It *sounds* ingenious."

"It was. Unfortunately, it took more time to take off than they had anticipated. A lot of wooing of big companies that move very slowly. My father started borrowing money to keep things afloat. Then a major company ordered thousands of units and they thought they'd made it. They secured another loan, went into large-scale production, only for the company to have second thoughts and the order fall through."

Her stomach dropped. "Oh, no."

His expression was grim. "It was the end. The death knell. They lost everything. We lost the house because my father had remortgaged it. The cars—all of it. My father started drinking, lapsed into a deep depression he never came out of."

"Why didn't he ask my father for help?" she queried, perplexed. "To start over?"

He rubbed a hand over his jaw. "He and Martino were the closest of friends, but they were also wildly competitive with one another. It was always who could execute the biggest deal, who could land the most beautiful woman. The rivalry continued when they started their own businesses. Except," he allowed, "Martino became massively successful, while my father's business failed."

"And he was too proud to ask for help."

He nodded. "He wouldn't speak to Martino or any of the others when they called. Refused to take handouts. My parents' marriage fell apart, and my mother moved back to California, where she's from."

Chloe gave him a horrified look. "She just *left* you with your father like that?"

His mouth twisted. "She said she hadn't signed on for that kind of a life."

She pressed a hand to her cheek, an ache forming deep in her chest. "How did you survive?"

"I left school and got a job. Went to classes at night. We lived in some pretty seedy places, but we made do."

And somehow, in the midst of it all, while he was taking care of his family, *holding it all together*, he had managed to get himself a scholarship to the university where he'd been completing his business degree when his father had died. Her father had reconnected with the boys at Leone's funeral and taken them under his wing.

She swallowed hard. It all made sense to her now. Nico's intense sense of honor. The laser focus with which he'd conducted his life, the *ruthless ambition* she had accused him of. He'd had no *choice*. He'd had two brothers and a father to take care of.

"I'm sorry," she said quietly. "That must have been so difficult, Nico."

He shrugged, the ice in his glass crackling in the still night air. "My brothers and I have always said it made us who we are. That we wouldn't *be* who we are were if not for what happened. So for that, I'm grateful."

But at what price? "Did you have any contact with your mother after she left?"

He shook his head. "She said she wanted to start a new life—that she couldn't do that with the baggage of her past along for the ride. She met and married Richard, the man you saw her with tonight, a year later."

Chloe drew in a breath. "I'm sure she didn't mean that."

"She meant it," he said flatly. "My father went

to see her—to plead with her to come back. She sent him away. The next time we heard from her was five years ago in New York. She came to apologize—to make amends for her mistakes. None of us wanted anything to do with her."

Her heart hitched. How could a mother just walk out on her children like that? It was inconceivable to her. But if there was anything she knew from her own experience in life, it was that people didn't always express what was deep inside themselves. They hid their hopes and fears. And maybe Nico's mother had been afraid. Maybe she'd simply been unable to cope with the way her life had disintegrated around her.

She wet her lips. "She seems to want to make amends, Nico. Can't you forgive her?"

"No," he rumbled, making her jump with the force of his response. "She walked out on us, Chloe. She *made* her decisions. It is ancient history, and I'm at peace with it."

He looked anything but. There was so much emotion on his face it hurt to look at him. He'd just worked his way through a good portion of a bottle of Scotch—Nico, whom she'd never seen have more than a couple of drinks. And now she knew why.

"Anger is not being at peace with it," she pursued. "Maybe you need to listen to her. To find forgiveness to find that peace in yourself."

He lapsed into silence. Made it clear the conversation was over as he drained his glass. "Go to bed," he said, without looking at her. "You've heard the whole sordid story now. No more to tell here."

"I'm not leaving you like this."

"I don't want to talk, Chloe."

She leaned back on the chair, palms planted in the cushion. "Fine, we won't talk."

He moved his gaze back to her. Hot, *deliberate*, it singed the curves of her breasts where the towel had fallen loose. "I don't want company either. Not when we both know what a bad idea that is."

Her stomach tipped upside down, a tremor moving through her. "Why?" she queried huskily. "We're consenting adults. You wanted to kiss me that night in my office during the perfume testing. I know you did."

He went still. "Which I didn't," he said harshly,

eyes on hers, "because I knew the insanity that it was. Which it *is*, Chloe."

She knew he was right. Knew she should keep up her guard when it came to him. But the severe, taut lines of his face held her spellbound. The redoubtable control he prized so greatly. Everything about him that did it for her like no other man ever had.

Did he still kiss the same way? As if he could do it all night? Would he make her turn to flame if he touched her again? Could she bear it if he never did?

She hugged her arms tight around herself. Felt a chill move through her that had nothing to do with the cool night air. She'd been cold for so long, *frozen* for such an eternity, she didn't remember what it felt like to be alive. To live in the moment. And suddenly she knew she couldn't do it one second longer. She wasn't going to leave him alone.

She lifted her chin. Trained her gaze on his. "Maybe I know it's crazy. Maybe I know I'm going to get burned. Maybe I haven't felt alive in so long I don't care."

A muscle jumped in his jaw. "You *should* care. I am not in the right headspace for this, Chloe."

But the heat in his smoky stare said otherwise. She was mesmerized by it as it melted her insides. By the chemical reaction that popped and fizzled between them. When she was in the lab, she manufactured reactions like this. With Nico, they were *real*. Out of her control. It made her pulse stutter, like she'd ingested some kind of dangerous drug.

"Come over here, then," he murmured, the hard lines of his face pure challenge. "If you're so sure of what you want."

He expected the invitation to frighten her off. She could tell from the look on his face. And for a moment it did, freezing all coherent thought. She sucked in a breath, delivered necessary oxygen to her brain. Knew in that moment this was the only opening she was ever going to get with Nico. She either seized it or wondered "what if" forever.

She shrugged her shoulders and let the towel fall to the chair. Got to her feet and walked over to him. He rested his head against the back of the chair and drank her in. Teeth buried in her lip, heart beating a jagged edge, she sat down on the inch of lounger beside him that was free. He was so gorgeous, so formidable in his disarray, sleeves rolled up to reveal corded, powerful forearms, heavy dark stubble dusting his jaw, her stomach went to dust.

His formidable control held even as his eyes turned to flame. He wasn't going to be the one to cross the line. It was going to be up to her to do it. And so she did, leaning forward and wrapping her fingers around his nape, absorbing the shift of tensile muscle and tendon beneath her fingertips as she brought her mouth down to his.

He didn't resist, but he didn't move to meet the kiss either. She found his lips with hers. Hard, betraying none of that inherent sensuality that was so much a part of him, she thought for a terrifying instant he was going to reject her. Then a soft curse escaped him, his arms clamped around her waist and he lifted her astride him, his hands cupping her bottom in his palms. She had just enough time to take a deep breath before he took her mouth in a hard, demanding kiss that slammed into her senses. *Demanded everything.*

As if it would make her run. As if he *wanted* her to run.

Instead, it made her skin burn. Her insides dissolve into liquid honey. The strong muscles in his neck flexed beneath her fingers as he angled his head to deepen the kiss. *Took*, until he seemed to be everywhere inside her, the taste of him dark and dangerous.

A groan tore itself from his throat. He shifted his hands to cup her jaw and slicked his tongue over the seam of her lips to gain entry. She opened for him, helpless to resist his sensual onslaught. Gasped as he stroked and licked his way inside her mouth, his hands at her jaw holding her in place for his delectation. As if he wanted to taste every centimeter of her. *Devour* her.

As intimate as the sexual act itself, *more*, the kiss made her stomach curl. She spread her palms against his chest, absorbing the latent strength that rested in every honed muscle. He tugged the clip from her hair and sent the heavy weight of it tumbling around her shoulders. Threaded his fingers through it and slowed the kiss down to a hot, languid seduction. The kind she remembered. The kind that went on forever.

His mouth left hers. Chloe murmured a protest, but then his lips were busy on her jaw, and then her neck, inducing those same brain-melting sensations. She shivered as he slid his hands from her hair down to cup her breasts. Tested their weight. Stroked his thumbs over the hard peaks, pushed taut by the night air. The shockingly pleasurable caress through the thin material of her swimsuit sent a wave of heat to her core.

"Nico," she breathed.

The tie of her bikini top gave way to the sharp tug of his fingers, and then there was only the delicious sensation of those strong, provocative hands on her bare flesh. The roll of her nipples between his fingers that made her moan deep in her throat. The heat of his ravenous gaze as he drank her in.

"You're beautiful," he said huskily. *Reverently.* "God, I've wanted to see you like this."

The look in his beautiful eyes made her fall apart inside. The heady male scent of him, the unmistakable musky smell of his desire, the iron-hard strength of his thighs beneath her were like seeing, *feeling*, the world in Technicolor again. She didn't think she could ever get enough of it.

She moved closer, seeking, *needing* more. Encountered hot, aroused male, burning her thighs through the material of his pants.

Oh. He was phenomenal. As into this as she was.

She melted into him, liquid with longing. Emboldened by the power she held over him. Whispered his name against his mouth.

"Chloe," he murmured, even as he took more of her weight in the hands he slid to her hips, rocking her against that most impressive part of him. "This is madness."

She bent her head and tugged his sensual bottom lip between her teeth. "I don't care."

His hand at her hips rocked her more firmly against him. Deeper, higher, the inferno raged until she was a slave to it. Until nothing existed except what he was making her feel. She whispered how much she wanted him in his ear. He told her how much he loved to hear her talk to him like that. How passionate, how honest her response had always been.

She gasped as he gripped her bottom tighter and raked her against the hard, aroused length of him, the wet, thin fabric of her swimsuit a delicious friction against the intoxicating steel beneath his pants.

Fire seared through her. She whimpered, moved against him, desperate, *hungry* for him to assuage the sweet ache between her thighs. For him to make her feel the things only he had ever been able to make her feel.

He angled her more intimately against him, giving her what she asked for. Ground himself against the aching center of her again and again until she sobbed her release in his ear.

"God, that is sexy," he murmured, a hand at her buttock holding her there, rotating his body against her until he'd wrung every last bit of pleasure out of her. "Give it all to me, sweetheart," he rasped. "All of it."

She collapsed against him, gasping for air. Shattered by the force of her release, incoherent with pleasure, rocked by the experience they had just shared. He had taken her apart, *dismantled* her. She felt exposed, *bare*, in a way she'd never experienced before.

She laid her head on his chest, listening to the

pounding of his heart as he held her. Soothed her. Brought her back down to earth with the smooth stroke of his hand across the bare skin of her back.

Nico wasn't actually sure when he'd lost his mind. It might have been the sight of Chloe climbing out of the pool, dripping wet in the sexy white bikini, all of that flawless, creamy skin on display. Or maybe it had been that first sweet touch of her mouth against his. The palpable vulnerability that clung to her like a second skin. But he hadn't been able to resist her. Or maybe it was himself he hadn't been able to refuse.

His breath a jagged blade in his chest, he clawed back control. Every male urge he had said to finish it, to take what he had always craved. To burn them both to oblivion in what followed, because surely it would be amazing. And completely, utterly *insane*.

He rubbed a palm against his temple, head hazy. What the hell was he doing? Was he really that weak that one kiss had been enough to dismantle the promises he'd made? To forget he was her boss...in a position of authority over her?

Or maybe it had been the whiskey, something he never should have started on. Another lapse in judgment.

He pulled in a breath, fury at his mother for starting this, disgust with himself, mixing in a potent brew. There was still time to assume control. He hadn't let things go *that* far.

Chloe pulled back to look at him, those devastating brown eyes of hers wide and shell-shocked, luminous with desire. "Nico," she murmured, reading the regret on his face. "Don't. I—"

He pulled her bikini top back into place, his hands fumbling over the ties as he redid them. Stood up, with her in his arms, and carried her inside. He didn't trust himself to talk with her half-dressed, and he sure as hell wasn't continuing what they'd started.

Taking the stairs to the second floor, he strode down the lamp-lit hallway and set her down outside her bedroom door. Leaning a hand against the wall, he pulled in a breath. Searched for something to say. But his lack of control when it came to her was such a lapse of judgment, any coherent thought dissolved in a red tide of fury directed solely at himself.

"That," he said harshly, "should not have happened."

She lifted her chin. "I wanted it to happen," she said evenly. "We have something, Nico. Ignoring it is only making it worse."

He gave her a withering look. "You are too vulnerable to have any idea what you're saying, and I'm too much of a son of a bitch not to have walked away. So *find* a way to get it out of your head, Chloe. For both our sakes."

CHAPTER SEVEN

NICO WOKE WITH a pounding headache. His alarm clock sounded like a fire engine, the sunshine pouring through the windows threatened to blind him, amplifying every throbbing beat of his head. Swiping at the clock with his hand, he silenced it. Sagged back against the pillows.

The events of the night before infiltrated his head. His mother showing up...that red-hot scene beside the pool with Chloe... *Merda.*

He hauled himself out of bed, showered and drank a gallon of the black coffee his housekeeper brewed for him, apparently not unused to the aftereffects of the whiskey phenomenon with Lazzero's hard-partying nights. The idea of walking for hours in the bright sunshine seemed an abhorrent idea, but as his golf game was with the president of the largest beauty retail chain in America, canceling was not an option.

He left the house with a thermos of coffee

tucked under his arm and a prayer of silent thanks Chloe was still in bed, because he could definitely wait until dinner to address *that* giant misstep.

Sliding into Lazzero's Porsche, he gunned the powerful car to life and followed Ocean Boulevard to his destination, a pristine stretch of blue ocean flanking his right.

You're angry, Nico... Perhaps you need to find forgiveness to find peace.

Chloe's words from the night before echoed through his head. He tightened his fingers around the steering wheel. Damned right he was angry. His mother had been a selfish, bitter creature who'd beguiled his father with her undeniable beauty, then made him pay every day of his life for getting her pregnant with him, even though, by all accounts, she'd been a dancer of mediocre talent who'd resorted to teaching to pay the bills.

Money had been the currency his mother had been willing to trade in. His father had sold what was left of his soul to give it to her. And when he'd eventually folded under the pressure, his mother had made him pay for failing to provide by walking out on New Year's Day.

Forgive her? He took a sip of his coffee. Wiped an infuriated palm across his jaw. *Never.* He was the one who'd had to pick up the pieces after the flashy-suited banker had left the Di Fiores' Greenwich Village home after delivering his instructions to repossess the house and everything in it. He was the one who'd taken one look at his father's grief-stricken face, his father who was *no longer there*, and assured his brothers that everything was going to be okay, when, in actual fact, he wasn't sure it would be at all.

He jammed his foot on the brake as a car cut in front of him. Hell yes, he was angry. *Furious* with his mother for approaching him like that when he'd made it clear he wanted nothing to do with her. He was also, he conceded, furious with himself for his own lack of control. For drowning himself in whiskey, pouring out the whole sordid story to Chloe and allowing himself to fall under the spell of a woman he'd vowed to keep his hands off.

A wave of bitter self-recrimination washed over him. He should have walked away. Instead, he'd put his hands on her, on everything he'd wanted from the first moment he'd seen her in that dress last night, and crossed the line. Had been so caught up in her uninhibited, innocent responses to his caresses, in the heat they'd generated together, he hadn't *thought*—he'd just taken.

Clearly he needed to find a better solution to his problem than the one he currently had. Luckily, he observed grimly, as he pulled into the perfectly manicured front entrance of one of Palm Beach's most prestigious golf clubs, he had eighteen holes to find it.

Find a way to get it out of your head.

Unfortunately, all Chloe *could* think about was last night with Nico as she brooded over a pot of coffee on the terrace in the morning sun. Hot, *erotic*, what they'd shared was indelibly burned into her head, never to be forgotten.

The way he'd *looked* at her…the things he'd said. It had been even more intense, more amazing, than her eighteen-year-old self had remembered.

Her skin burned, a flush spreading from her chest up to her cheeks, singeing them with a fiery heat. Nico had been as caught up in the moment as she had been. As if he'd been giving in to his feelings, too. As if he hadn't been able to help himself. It validated everything she'd thought about them all those years ago. As if that had been the truth of them.

To know she could affect him like that, that she could make him lose control, shook her to her toes.

And then he'd walked away. *Again.*

She sank her teeth into her lip. Stared out at the sparkling, azure sea. She had seduced Nico into kissing her. Pushed him over the edge. With the hopes that what? He would take her to bed? That he would say to hell with the consequences, of which there were many, admit that what they had was special and be so lost in the moment he wouldn't be able to resist her?

Her stomach turned over on a low, antagonized pull. He had *confided* in her. That meant something, because Nico never talked to anyone. Now she knew the experiences that had shaped him— why he never formed lasting attachments with women. Because he didn't *trust* them.

Which should be a giant, blinking yellow caution sign. One she should heed for her own self-preservation. Instead, she felt exhilarated.

Invigorated. Alive. She'd put herself out there, gone after what she'd wanted for the first time in her life, and it had been *amazing.* And that was where her thought processes began and ended.

She spent the day on the beach, until the sun slanted lower in the sky, Nico's return from his golf game imminent. Then she peeled herself off the lounger and headed up to the house to shower and change for dinner.

Sliding on a short, baby-doll-style dress in moss green silk that hinted at her curves in the subtlest of ways, she caught her hair up in a simple high ponytail, applied a light dusting of makeup, then made her way downstairs, her stomach tight with nerves.

Nico was waiting for her on the terrace. His skin tanned an even darker brown from the day in the sun, muscular body clad in faded jeans that clung to his powerful thighs and a black T-shirt that did the same for his amazing abs, aviator sunglasses on his face, he was drool worthy in a way that stopped her heart in its tracks.

Also vastly intimidating.

"How was your day?" he asked evenly, clearly back in full Nico control.

"Lovely." She could play this game, too. "Yours?"

"It was a good networking day." He tipped his head to the side. "I thought we might have a drink before dinner."

A good idea. They could have a mature, honest conversation about last night so her stomach would stop crawling with nerves.

He poured her the glass of white wine she requested. Fixed himself a sparkling water with lime and leaned back against the bar, cradling it between his fingers. Chloe sank her teeth into her lip.

Was he going to take the sunglasses off or was she going to have to guess at what he was feeling?

As if he'd read her mind, he reached up and slid the glasses off. His cool gray gaze met hers. "I think we should talk about last night."

"Agreed." She took a sip of her wine with a hand that trembled ever so slightly. Eyed him.

"It can't happen again." Flat. Definitive.

"Why?"

His gaze narrowed. "Would you like me to list the reasons? Because I am your boss. Because you are my responsibility, Chloe. Because it would be a big, giant mess."

She shook her head. "That's an excuse, and you know it. Yes, we have to work together, but our current situation is already complicating that. As for you being my boss," she said, shrugging, "that's semantics really. I *own* Evolution, Nico. It's my company. So there is no power imbalance between us. Which only," she concluded, "leaves us with the real issue here—that you keep walking away and why."

"I don't sleep with the people I work with," he said matter-of-factly, "regardless of any power imbalance. It's a policy of mine. And you *are* my responsibility, that's a fact. I am your regent."

"And last night?" she prompted, lifting a brow. "What was that? Because I would say we well and truly crossed the line."

A muscle twitched in his jaw. "It was a...*slip* on my part."

Humiliation fired her cheeks, the clear regret in his voice activating that deep-rooted insecurity she did so well. "Because I threw myself at you again?" she suggested huskily. "A *pity* kiss to get me off your back?"

His lashes lowered in a hooded gaze. "You know that's not true."

"Then what *was* it?" She shook her head, frustration stinging her skin. "I'm going a little crazy here, Nico. I think I'm imagining things one minute, then I'm sure I'm not the next. You're hot, then you're cold. Which is it?"

A flicker of antagonism marred his deadly gray cool. "What would you have me say?" he bit out. "That I wanted to make love to you last night? That I was one step short of carrying you to my bed and taking everything you were offering? Because we both know that I was. And where would that have gotten us?"

Her insides dissolved, the sensory impact behind his words slamming into her brain with visceral effect. How *close* to the edge he'd been with that iron-clad control of his.

"To a place of honesty," she murmured, wrapping her arms around herself. "What you said to me the night of the board meeting. About me hiding from you. Hiding from myself. You were right, Nico. I have been. Because you make me feel things I've never felt with anyone else. Things I want to explore—things I'm *terrified* to explore. But by far, my worse crime has been hiding from myself. Denying what I want and need in life because I'm too afraid to go after it. So last night I did."

His eyes widened imperceptibly, before he schooled his expression back into one of those inscrutable looks. "You don't want me, Chloe. The relationships I have with women are short and transactional. A few enjoyable nights spent together, a dinner or two thrown in and then I walk away. There are *rules* to it."

"That's right," she murmured, voice dripping with sarcasm. "Your *rules*. Those personal *entanglements* you avoid like the plague. Funny, when I've never asked for that from you. Maybe you should ask yourself what *you* are hiding from."

His jaw hardened. "*Chloe.* Stop pushing."

"Why? Because we might finally get at the truth here?"

He muttered an oath. Strode to the edge of the railing to stand looking out at the ocean, a long silence passing between them. "I made a promise to your father to take care of you. I won't break it."

She blinked. Followed him to the railing. "What promise?"

He turned to face her. "Last spring, your father developed a cough. He thought nothing of it, but when it persisted for a few weeks, he went to see his doctor. He was diagnosed with incurable lung cancer. Told he had two years to live."

Her breath whooshed from her lungs. "*Lung cancer?* He didn't smoke."

"He did back in his Wall Street days. He said it was a bad habit that had finally caught up with him."

Her brain struggled to process what he was telling her. That step back her father had taken…his pristine will and succession planning. It all made sense now. *He had known he was going to die.* That he would not be around to guide Evolution.

"I don't understand," she said numbly. "Why didn't he tell us?"

His gaze softened. "He didn't want to worry you. He told your mother, of course. Me—because he wanted to get the succession of the company in order—to ensure Juliette and you girls were taken care of before he made the news public. Which he wasn't going to do until he had to because he felt the rumor and speculation would be harmful to the company."

Hot emotion bubbled up inside her, threatening to spill over her carefully contained edges. "You should have told me," she rasped. "I could have come home from Paris. I could have spent that time with them. Time I will never get back."

"Your father didn't want that," he said evenly. "He wanted you to live your life. He wanted to see you fly. It was his *wish*. I couldn't just circumvent it."

"Yes, you could have." She threw the words at him, hands tightening into fists by her sides. "How many openings have I given you to tell me this, Nico? I *knew* a piece of the puzzle was missing, I *asked* you, and still you didn't tell me. Where is that trust you were demanding? I'm not seeing it."

He pushed away from the railing. Reached for her. She stepped back, eyes on his.

"I was trying to protect you," he said quietly. "You've had enough blows. I needed you focused on saving Evolution with me."

"And you didn't think I could have *handled* it?" She threw him an infuriated look. "Why does everyone think I need my decisions made for me? Do you think I'm that delicate that I can't handle the truth?" She waved a hand at him. "I'm a grown woman, Nico. You keep telling me to have confidence in who I am—to *believe* in who I am—but you won't trust me enough to make my own decisions."

He regarded her silently for a moment. "You're grieving, Chloe. It makes you vulnerable."

Vulnerable. That word she was beginning to hate. "What about my uncle? Does he know?"

He shook his head. "Your father knew how badly Giorgio wanted to run Evolution. That it was going to be a blow that he hadn't chosen him. He was going to tell him at the right time. Position it the right way."

"Instead, he died, leaving Giorgio furious with you and confused about why my father did what he did. A *rogue element.*"

"Yes."

And he, because he was rock-solid Nico, impenetrable in a storm, had taken everything she and Giorgio had thrown at him because he was uncompromising when it came to his sense of honor to those he was indebted to. And he was indebted to her father. He had given Nico a second lease on life, and he would never forget it. Nor would he break his promises when it came to her.

Once again, her choices were being taken away from her.

She pressed her palms to her temples, her brain too full to think. Except for the one thing in her head that *was* crystal clear. "Can we just establish one point?" she murmured, echoing his words from the night before. "I am not too *vulnerable* to handle what happened between us last night. And I don't need you taking care of me, so you can absolve yourself of that responsibility, too, along with your propensity to make decisions for me. I no longer require it."

"Chloe—"

Numb, furious, she turned and headed for the stairs to the beach.

"Where are you going?" he fired after her.

"For a walk. I'm too angry with you right now to be in your presence."

She flew down the stairs. Kicked off her shoes and started walking, the sand still warm beneath her feet, the sun a kaleidoscope of shattered gold on the horizon.

Anger flared inside her, hot and wild, as she walked, toes sinking into the sand. At her father for keeping the truth from her. For taking away her chance to spend that time with him and her mother. For taking away any chance she might have had with Nico. At Nico for not telling her the truth.

Hot tears filled her eyes, blurred her vision. She sank down on the concrete break wall and covered her face with her hands. She wasn't ever going to get a chance to say goodbye…to tell her parents how much they'd meant to her. That phone call in Paris on her way home from work, the one that had seemed far too surreal, far too unfair, far too *sudden*, had been it.

A tear slipped down her cheek. Then another, until they were a steady stream of hot warmth, the salt staining her lips. And once started, she couldn't stop, all of the emotion she'd had locked up inside her escaping on a wave of despair, until her sobs robbed her of her breath, shattered her from the inside out, the pain in her chest nothing compared with the one in her heart.

* * *

Nico told himself to leave Chloe alone. That this had been a long time coming. That the wise, *rational* course of action would be for him to give her the space she'd asked for—to allow her to get it all out without complicating things further with an even deeper emotional attachment to a woman he couldn't have. But he couldn't seem to do it, her raw sobs squeezing tight fingers around his heart.

He took a seat beside her on the wall, picked her up and pulled her onto his lap, cradling her against his chest. She stiffened, as if she might resist, then another sob racked through her and she melted into him, her tears soaking his T-shirt.

He smoothed a hand down her back and murmured words of comfort against her silky hair. Long minutes passed, until finally her sobs turned into hiccuping big breaths and she went quiet against him.

The rhythmic sound of the rolling surf stretched between them, the sun a fiery, yellow ball as it sank into the sea.

"I want them back," she murmured against his chest. "I miss them every day."

A strange ache unearthed itself behind his rib cage. "I know," he said softly, tucking a stray strand of her hair behind her ear. "I do, too. But you have to let them go. And when you do," he promised, pressing a hand against her chest, "you'll find they're *here*."

She looked up at him, eyes twin glimmering mahogany pools. "Is your father there? For you?"

He nodded. "The man he was. Not the man he became."

Her gaze darkened. "I'm glad." She exhaled a long breath. Swiped the tears from her cheeks. "I guess it's just frightening, you know? They were always there for me when life got bumpy. A phone call away. *My safety net.*"

"You don't need it," he said softly, eyes on hers. "You've got this, Chloe. You're proving it."

She caught her bottom lip between her teeth. Something unfurled beneath his skin. A need to comfort, to soothe, to *touch*. To protect her as had always been his urge. To take her amazing mouth with his and make everything better. But a stronger part of him knew it for the mistake it would be. That one more taste of her would be his undoing.

He wasn't *hiding* from his feelings for her—he simply knew his capabilities. He didn't have the capacity to take on another person's happiness, had had enough of that for a lifetime.

"Nico—" She reached up and smoothed her fingers over his jaw, her brown eyes luminous.

He caught her fingers in his. "Dinner's ready," he murmured. "I think we should go up."

Her mouth firmed, eyes cooling. Sliding off his lap, she brushed the sand from her dress. Set off up the stairs to the house, without looking back at him, her spine ramrod straight.

Bene. They were back to her hating him. Him knowing it was the better way. At least it was a status quo he knew and understood.

CHAPTER EIGHT

CHLOE SPENT THE week back at work doing her best to focus on the frantic preparations for the Vivre launch rather than her roller-coaster weekend in Palm Beach with Nico. But she found it almost impossible to do so.

Knowing why her father had done what he had done had made everything seem more confusing rather than less, because that meant Nico *was* the honorable man she'd always thought him to be. It meant she'd been wrong about everything when it came to him, not helpful when he'd taken any chance of *them* happening off the table.

She couldn't change the fact that she'd been wrong about so many things, nor could she do anything about Nico's overinflated sense of honor she loved and hated at the same time. About the fact that he had distanced himself from her ever since Palm Beach. What she could do was make sure Vivre took the world by storm, to *fly* as her father had wanted her to do.

With her campaign set to go live in just a couple of weeks on November 15, everything was falling into dizzying place. She'd travel to Europe to meet with the regional teams next week to put the final pieces in place for the launches in London and Paris. Then she'd come back to New York to launch the campaign at the Evolution Christmas party, with Be on sale to the public the day after, in a splashy launch with Lashaunta.

They were operating on the razor's edge, but they were pulling it off.

She gave her phone a cursory glance as she waited in line for her midmorning latte. Almost dropped her purse at the photo that came up in her news feed.

Juggling her bag and phone in one hand, she scrambled for money with the other, found some dollar bills and shoved them at the barista. Stepping to the side to wait, she scanned the cutline of the photo of Eddie Carello and his current girlfriend emblazoned across the front page of a popular gossip site.

Eddie Carello Enjoys Wild Night in the Bahamas!

Things got a bit out of hand on the weekend at a luxury hotel in Nassau, where Hollywood heartthrob Eddie Carello was enjoying a wild post-concert party.

A hotel suite was allegedly trashed during the incident, which apparently caught Carello in flagrante delicto amid a supposed ménage à trois with girlfriend Camille Hayes and a waitress from the hotel.

The ruckus began when guests complained about the noise levels in the hotel and staff were dispersed to handle the complaint.

When asked about the incident, Carello's spokesperson replied that "the whole thing has been overblown and people shouldn't believe everything they hear."

Meanwhile, Hollywood's hottest star seems to have upped his outrageous antics in advance of his new movie, Score, *giving everyone something to talk about around the water cooler this morning.*

Nooo.

Chloe clutched her phone in one hand, latte in the other and hoofed it back to work. She was out of breath by the time she reached Mireille's office. Her sister, who was on the phone, gestured her into the seat opposite her. Chloe threw her phone on Mireille's desk and collapsed into the chair, attempting not to panic.

Her sister finished the call. Picked up Chloe's phone and scanned the story. Started to laugh. "Well, you knew," she drawled, "he wasn't lily-white. But that was the attraction, right? He's a rebel—the new James Dean. A perfect fit for Soar."

"Yes, but—" Chloe gestured at the phone "—isn't this *bad* PR?"

"PR is rarely bad." Mireille sat back in her chair and crossed one elegant leg over the other. "If anything, this is going to make him a hotter property. I wouldn't be surprised if they manufactured this for the buzz. Although," she conceded, "he doesn't need it."

"I don't *want* him doing things like this," Chloe said worriedly. "He was fine the way he was."

Mireille lifted a shoulder. "Not much you can do about it. If you had a major sponsorship that he was riding on, you might have something to say about it. But in your case, he's doing you a favor. Sit tight," she advised, "let it burn itself out. The news will be on to something else by the weekend."

Since Mireille was the expert, and she knew nothing about these things, Chloe took a deep breath and sat back in her chair. "Okay."

Mireille fixed her with a speculative look. "Any reason Nico bit your head off in the meeting this morning?"

Chloe, who'd planned on keeping her mouth shut about the whole thing, found her cheeks heating. "I kissed him."

Mireille sat up in her chair, eyes wide. "I'm sorry. Can you repeat that?"

She bit her lip. "I kissed Nico…in Palm Beach."

Her sister stared at her. "Forgive me. I'm still stuck at the part where you just said you kissed your boss."

Chloe scowled. "You are not being helpful."

Mireille smiled. "Oh, come on, Chloe, it's about time. In fact, I'm not sure how it hasn't happened sooner. You two have had a thing for each other as long as I can remember. Santo and I always joke about it."

Chloe gave her a horrified look. "You and Santo joke about it?"

Mireille waved a hand at her. "Why the long face, then? What happened?"

Her lashes lowered. "He told me it was a mistake. That it never should have happened."

"Because you are his responsibility. Because he's Nico." Her sister shrugged. "Nico was never going to be a forever kind of guy, you knew that. He's a night-to-remember guy. If you're suicidal enough to want that after everything he did to you, seduce him again and do it right this time. Or find someone else to get over him with."

She didn't want anyone else. That was her problem. She never had.

The passion she and Nico had shared that night flickered through her head—an intoxicating, irresistible memory that refused to be extinguished. A surge of determination coursed through her. Maybe she was done letting everyone else make her decisions for her. Maybe it was time for her to convince Nico this *was* her decision to make.

* * *

Nico waited until he and Jerry Schumacher, the most senior member of Evolution's board, had finished an excellent dinner at Jerry's favorite Manhattan steakhouse, including a superior bottle of amarone, before he broached the subject of the current thorn in his side.

"Giorgio Russo," he said bluntly. "How big of a problem is he?"

Jerry sat back in his leather chair and swirled the dark red wine in his glass. "There are a few board members who have always been sympathetic to him. Maybe he's picked up another couple of late with his campaign. But your support is solid, Nico. Deliver a good Christmas and you'll silence him."

He slid a file across the table to Nico. "The names you asked for."

Nico slid the folder into his briefcase. "*Grazie.* I owe you one." He took a deep sip of his wine. Contemplated Jerry as he set the glass down. "Christmas will be good. We are going big with Vivre—a fifty-million-dollar launch with the A-list celebrities Chloe presented at the meeting. It's going to put Evolution back on the map."

A smile twisted Jerry's mouth. "You never were the faint-hearted type, were you? A chip off the old block."

Nico inclined his head. Refused to reveal how the comparison burrowed under his skin. Jerry had known his father during his Wall Street days when Leone Di Fiore had been known for his big, risky deals—suicidal, some had liked to call them. But he'd always pulled them off. Until he hadn't with the most important one of them all— the one he'd gambled his life savings on.

"The signature fragrances are what the company was built around," Nico pointed out. "They're what's going to bring the company back to life."

A rueful look painted itself across Jerry's face. "My wife sure as hell is a zealot. She's mad about that damn perfume. What is it… Live?"

"Be," Nico corrected.

"Be, right." Jerry frowned, his bushy, white brows drawing together. "Wasn't one of Chloe's celebrities that Eddie character? The Hollywood guy?"

Nico's lips curved. "Yes. He has a big movie coming out in December. Perfect for the launch."

Jerry reached down and scavenged around in his briefcase. Pulled out a newspaper. A tabloid, Nico noted as Jerry handed it to him.

"You buy this stuff?"

The retired CEO gave him a sheepish look. "My wife. She made me promise to bring it home. Apparently, it was all over the radio this morning."

Nico scanned the story on Eddie Carello and his wild threesome in Nassau. He would have been amused by the actor's exploits if he wasn't the cornerstone of his fifty-million-dollar Vivre ad campaign. It was a sensational piece, no doubt about it. Who knew how much of it was true? But he'd seen enough Hollywood stars implode under their own egos that it worried him.

"It will sell lots of perfume," he said to Jerry.

He headed back to the office after he'd dropped Jerry at home. Sought out Giorgio, who was still working. The older man greeted him with his usual lazily satisfied attitude until Nico flipped open the file Jerry had given him and listed off the names of the board members Giorgio had been courting. When Giorgio sputtered and attempted to defend himself, Nico closed the folder and slid it back into his briefcase.

"Food for thought," he told the arrogant, ego-centric fool, "while you consider your future within the company. Because one more errant move on your part and you'll be out of a job."

Leaving him to scramble in a web of his own making, Nico sought out his second, perhaps bigger problem.

Chloe wasn't in the lab when he checked there, the one other person who was telling him she was up in the lounge, screening her promotional spots.

He found her curled up on the sofa in the lounge, watching Eddie's commercial, a pizza box and an assortment of soda cans in front of her. Dressed in black leggings and a figure-hugging sweater, the high boots she'd been wearing kicked off, her hair loose around her shoulders, she looked sexy and takeable.

His inability to forget that hot encounter by the pool appeared to be his third problem.

She eyed him. Sat up straight, picked up the remote control and put the video on pause.

"I just informed your uncle I will fire him if he doesn't cease his smear campaign."

Her eyes widened. "You can't *fire* him. He owns part of the company."

"Your father gave me the green light to do so."

She was silent for a moment, eyes on his. "He loves Evolution, Nico. Tell him the truth."

"He'll find another reason to perpetuate his antics. He has a choice. He can make it." He threw the tabloid he'd purchased on the coffee table. "That discussion is closed. *This* one, however, is a problem."

She glanced at the tabloid. Back at him. "I talked to Mireille. She says there's no reason to panic. That, if anything, this will amplify the buzz around Eddie. Make him even more popular."

"Maybe so," he agreed. "But this is a fifty-million-dollar ad campaign, Chloe. We have staked the future of the company on it. Eddie Carello is a loose cannon...a wild card. What if his behavior amplifies instead of de-escalates?"

"It *will* die down," she insisted. "Mireille thinks it's even possible his handlers manufactured this as movie publicity."

"Not something I want to gamble the Evolution brand on." He blew out a breath. Shoved his hands in his pockets. "I think we should cut him. The other three can carry the campaign."

Chloe gaped at him. Rolled to her feet and came to stand in front of him. "We can't throw Eddie away. He's the anchor of the campaign, Nico—marketing gold. He is going to make the Evolution brand *relevant* again."

"He's too much of a risk," he countered flatly. "Remember when I said not one thing can go wrong with this campaign? I meant *not one thing*, Chloe. This is asking for trouble."

She crossed her arms over her chest. "You're overreacting."

"I am not overreacting. There are no second chances with this. This campaign goes south, so does the company. It's that simple."

"I *know* that." Fire flared in her eyes. "I had the same reaction as you when I walked in today. Then Mireille set me straight. *You* are the one who has been telling me I need to listen to the experts. To lean on my team when I need to. To *learn* from them. Well, I have, and Mireille is telling me it's fine, so it's fine."

He closed his eyes. She pressed the advantage.

"The others can't carry Soar. It's a men's fragrance. Eddie needs to. He *is* Soar."

He bit back the response that came to his lips. To *order* her to cut Eddie, because that was what he would have done. He *had* counseled her to consult the experts. Which she had, and Mireille, whom he trusted, had weighed in. So how could he turn around and veto them both?

Perhaps he *was* overreacting. And maybe he didn't know what the hell he was doing anymore. He only knew his head wasn't entirely clear when it came to her.

He had removed a piece of her clothing in Palm Beach. Had been imagining doing it again ever since. Except *all of it* this time.

His mouth thinned, a throb unearthing itself at his temples. He was starting to think *he* had been the naive one to think he could separate the personal from the professional when it came to Chloe because he didn't seem to be doing a very good job of it either.

He brought his back teeth together. Followed his own advice and went with the experts. "Call Eddie's agent. Tell him to tone it down."

She blinked. Nodded. "I will. Thank you."

He gestured toward the TV. "Are you almost finished here? It's late. I can drive you home."

"No, I have more to do. I—" She jammed her teeth into her lip and stared at him.

"What?"

"You're avoiding me and you're snapping at me in meetings."

Caught utterly off guard, he kept his face impassive. "I am not avoiding you."

"You canceled three of our meetings this week, Nico."

"I am busy running the company, in case you hadn't noticed."

She pursed her lips, long dark lashes fanning down over her cheeks. "That's what you said to me about me hiding in Paris. I think you're doing the same with us."

She was right. Absolutely right. He *had* been avoiding her, because his lust was a problem. But he wasn't about to admit it.

"You're imagining it," he said blithely.

"Am I?" Her gaze remained unwavering on his. "Are you punishing me for what happened in Palm Beach?"

"Yes," he agreed, voice heavy with sarcasm,

"I am punishing you, Chloe. As we make fifty-million-dollar decisions together."

Her gaze dropped to her stocking-clad feet for a moment before she looked back up at him. "I can't get what happened that night at the pool out of my head. The way it was between us. I don't think either of us can. I think we need to address it."

His gaze narrowed. "*What* exactly are you suggesting?"

"I want to explore what we have. I want to know what that kind of passion feels like. No strings attached."

His jaw dropped. "You're suggesting we have an affair?"

"Yes."

His head pounded, like a grenade ready to go off. Was she really standing there, calmly suggesting they have an affair? The no-strings-attached type he specialized in? She was *insane*.

Except was it really that insane? A part of him knew it hadn't been the whiskey that had made him cross the line that night in Palm Beach. That he'd crossed it because he'd wanted to. Because he wanted *her*. Because it had been a long time in the making. But that didn't mean Chloe's was a sane solution.

"We can't maintain the status quo," she murmured, pressing forward in the silence.

"Perhaps not," he rasped. "But I can assure you that *now* is not the right time for this discussion."

"When do you think might be?"

"Not now." He stooped and picked up his briefcase. "Go to Paris, Chloe. Make this launch happen. And keep that damn actor of yours on a leash."

CHAPTER NINE

PARIS WAS A BLUR.

Nico's warning to execute the launch without a hitch echoing in her head, Chloe threw herself into the final preparations with the regional teams in Europe, visiting Paris first to ensure the pop-up store on the Champs-élysées was gleaming and ready to go. She stayed at her apartment she'd kept in the sixth arrondissement while she was there, and had dinner with the team and Estelle at one of her favorite cafés to run through the launch event logistics.

Funnily enough, she didn't feel homesick for her adopted home like she'd been sure she would. She found herself at peace instead. She was doing what she was destined to do, there was no longer any question in her mind. And she *knew* she could do it now.

Her meetings with the London team went off seamlessly, as well. She flew back to New York just in time for the Evolution Christmas party. Always scheduled during mid-November, it served as the official kickoff to the holiday season—the most important sales season for Evolution. After the party for the company's employees, customers and partners that evening, Be would be launched to the public the next day with an appearance by Lashaunta in Times Square.

Chloe was running on an adrenaline-induced high by the time she arrived at her town house to dress for the party with Mireille, a Christmas tradition. It was only when Mireille waved Carrie Mayer's newspaper feature at her that her stomach sank.

What if it was awful? Mireille's deadpan expression wasn't giving anything away.

Heart pounding in her chest, Chloe sank down in an armchair with the paper and took a deep breath.

Scent of a Woman
by Carrie Mayer

When I sat down with Chloe Russo, daughter of legendary American perfumer Juliette Russo, I wasn't sure what to expect. A teen-

age phenomenon who launched her own fragrance at seventeen, she has remained out of the public eye for much of her life.

I wondered if she would have her mother's intense charisma...or perhaps she would be the opposite, languishing under the weight of the expectations placed upon her to fill the shoes of a woman who burned as one of the industry's brightest stars.

Instead, I found a bit of an enigma. A warm, engaging woman who entranced me from the moment I sat down. Who captivated me with her passion for her calling. A woman whose talent clearly stands on its own.

There is, however, clearly a message behind her new perfume line, Vivre, that perhaps echoes the struggle she has waged to forge that identity. And that, according to Russo, is to simply "be." To let your spirit define you. To know the only limitations in life are the ones you place on yourself.

A tear slipped down her cheek as she read the rest. Then another. They were a steady stream by the time she put down the paper and her sister pulled her to her feet for a hug.

184 CHRISTMAS AT THE TYCOON'S COMMAND

"You've done it, sweetie. Mamma would be so proud. This is your night to shine."

"Oh, no." Chloe pulled out of her arms. "I forgot to buy a dress in all this insanity."

"That's what you have me for." Her sister threw her a satisfied smile as she plucked one off the back of a chair. *"I knew you would. Voilà."*

Chloe tried on the black dress her sister presented. Halter-style, it had straps that crisscrossed around her neck, leaving her shoulders and much of her back bare. Body hugging, it fit her like a glove, highlighting every dip and curve.

It was sophisticated, *daring*. Chloe pursed her lips. "I'm not sure I can pull it off."

"You're the only one who *could* pull it off." Mireille waved a dismissive hand at her. "You wear all those French creations I could never hope to fit into. It's going to make Nico's eyes bug out of his head."

Butterflies swooped low in her stomach. Was that what she wanted? She'd been so busy since she'd left for Europe, she and Nico hadn't broached the subject of *them*. She wondered if she was crazy to have even proposed it. But she knew in her heart it *was* what she wanted, this chance to be with him. So she was letting the chips fall where they may.

Except where were they going to fall? It was almost painful, the waiting.

She slipped on decadently high black heels and the ornate triangular onyx earrings Mireille had given her for Christmas last year, while her sister dressed in a fire-engine-red gown that fit her vibrant personality. And then they were ready for Evolution's big night.

Restored to its original glory in 2008, The Grand Ballroom of the Plaza, which had once played host to Truman Capote's famous Black and White Ball, had retained its glorious neoclassical decor with its grand arches and stunning massive antique chandeliers.

Tonight, as the setting for Evolution's annual Christmas party, the ballroom echoed that classic black-and-white theme, with the invitations, catering and decor all reflecting the elegant color scheme, because it had been Juliette Russo's favorite.

High black vases brimming with white lilies graced the tables scattered around the room, champagne with blackberries as its adornment was the opening cocktail and the massive Christmas tree in the center of the room glittered in cream and ebony.

With the Vivre campaign playing on screens placed discreetly around the room, the stunning, evocative creative adding the perfect touch of Hollywood glamour to the evening, it was simply *magical*. And with Eddie and Lashaunta in attendance tonight, it was also Manhattan's hottest ticket in town.

Chloe and Mireille had arrived before the guests to make sure everything was perfect, as their mother had always done. But the events team had outdone themselves, every festive piece in place. Relaxing with the hotel manager, they chatted about some of the legendary parties that had taken place in the ballroom as they waited for the guests to arrive.

Chloe wasn't exactly sure when she sensed Nico's presence in the room. It was instinctive with her, this awareness of him that seemed to reach soul deep. But when she turned around, he still took her breath away.

Dressed in an elegant black tux, his dark hair

slicked back from his face, his fabulous, severe bone structure cast into harsh relief, he looked sleek, lithe and outrageously good. *Dangerous* in a way that sent a convulsive shiver up her spine. Because two weeks away hadn't lessened her attraction to him. It had only intensified it.

Greeting both her and Mireille, he pressed a kiss to Mireille's cheeks first. When her sister discreetly faded away to "check on a piece of missing decor," Nico set his gaze on Chloe. The not-so-subtle heat singed her skin as he moved it down over her body. Lingered at the bare sweep of her shoulders, the length of leg, before he brought his perusal back up to her face.

"You look stunning," he murmured, his husky voice sending another shiver through her as he bent his head and brushed his lips to both of her cheeks. She sucked in a breath at the electric contact, any air she'd managed to consume lodged somewhere in her chest as he straightened and set a silvery gaze on her.

"Did Mireille show you Carrie's piece?"

"Yes." Her chest tightened, as if a fist had wrapped itself around it. He'd been there for her all along. Not just now, but during the hardest months of her life when her parents had died, managing things in the background. *Always there.* She just hadn't seen it.

She wasn't sure she could articulate how much it meant to her. But she tried. "Thank you," she said, eyes on his. "For believing in me. For supporting me. It means everything."

His eyes darkened to a gunmetal gray. "You did it, Chloe, not me. I simply kept you on track."

"But you put your faith in me. It was what I needed."

"I put my faith in your *talent*." A smile flitted across his mouth. "Now we just need to sell some perfume."

And wasn't that the fifty-million-dollar question? "We will," she said, more confidently than she felt.

His smile deepened. "Let's go greet the guests, then. They're starting to arrive."

Santo rested a hand against one of the pillars flanking the ballroom, his eyes on the elegant black-and-white-clad, bejeweled crowd.

"Quite a party," he murmured. "Lashaunta and

Eddie Carello in attendance…the mayor, even. This must put even *you* in a festive mood."

Nico ignored the gibe. He hated Christmas. Had ever since their mother had walked out on New Year's Day. It had been all he could do to make it through the elaborate Christmases at the Russos' house in Great Neck without climbing out the window.

"It's a good party," he acknowledged, with a tip of his head. "Your ex was at the bar earlier with her jet-set crew."

"I saw her. She did your print campaign this year, didn't she?"

Nico nodded. Santo's ex—a model scaling the heights of superstardom—was still crazy about his brother. He couldn't figure their relationship out. Neither could his brother, it seemed, the way it went back and forth like a Ping-Pong match.

Nico cocked a brow. "What did she think of you and your reporter date?"

Santo lifted a shoulder. "Not so thrilled. But a relationship can't just be about lust. I'm looking for a soul mate."

Nico's mouth twisted. "Do you actually *believe* the things you say?"

"Si." Santo gave him an unconcerned look. "I believe love exists. I simply think it's hard to find."

Santo, Nico mused, was an eternal optimist. How he managed that particular attribute after watching their parents' bitter wreck of a marriage disintegrate was beyond him. At least Lazzero, currently off on business in Brazil, had no interest in Santo's concept of eternal love. Lazzero was even more cynical than he.

"Speaking of beautiful women," Santo said, nodding his head toward Chloe, who was dancing with Eddie in the center of the room, "this is certainly her night. All the big stars repping her perfumes...she must be on top of the world."

"She is." There was a curious tightness in his chest, a pride, he told himself, in everything Chloe had accomplished. She'd become the strong, confident woman he'd always known she could be, taking on her demons with courage and slaying them one at a time. Had demonstrated a core of steel as she'd made an impossible campaign timeline work, refusing to let any setbacks faze her.

He'd be a liar if he said she didn't affect him, because she did. She always had. And perhaps Santo was right. Perhaps she didn't need his brand of protection anymore. Perhaps she was capable of knowing what she wanted when it came to them. Perhaps burning this thing out between them *was* the right answer. But could she handle an affair with him? Or would it make even more of a mess of the situation than it already was?

Eddie bent his head and said something in Chloe's ear that made her laugh. Her bright, vibrant smile kicked Nico right in the chest. He'd missed her these past couple of weeks she'd been in Europe—her quick wit, that razor-sharp brain, the way she challenged him at every turn.

If he were being honest, he'd admit he was fighting a losing battle over something he'd wanted for far too long.

Chloe's head was spinning from all the dancing and conquering she'd done. More than one journalist had pulled her aside to tell her how much they loved her perfumes. Jerry Schumacher's wife had gushed to her about Be and how much she adored it, and the silent auction of her yet-to-become-available complete set of Vivre perfumes was going for thousands.

Eddie and Lashaunta had been a huge hit, Eddie, thankfully, on his best behavior tonight. It couldn't have gone any better. Except, of course, if Nico had danced with her. Which he hadn't. Once again, he'd danced with everyone *but* her.

"It's almost midnight," Mireille murmured. "You need to put the star on the tree."

Chloe's stomach knotted. Putting the star on the Christmas tree had always been her mother's job—the symbolic kickoff to the most exciting, important time of the year for Evolution. She knew it was her job now, she just wasn't sure she could do it.

But Nico, true to his usual, impeccably punctual self, appeared then. The knot in Chloe's stomach grew as they walked toward the center of the room. "I'm not sure I can do this," she murmured.

"Yes, you can," he countered firmly. "I thank everyone for their contributions this year and you stick the star on the tree. Nothing to it."

Except when they got to the center of the room

and Nico had quieted the crowd to give his remarks, her heart was beating so loudly it echoed in her ears and her knees felt like jelly.

However was she going to climb that ladder? She could feel five hundred sets of eyes on her as she toed off her shoes and stepped onto the first rung, Nico spotting her as she went. Climbing to the top, she affixed the beautiful white star to the tree with trembling fingers. Felt something in her heart break. She thought she might have finally said goodbye.

Nico caught her hand in his as she got to the bottom of the ladder. "Put on your shoes," he said. "I haven't danced with you yet."

If she'd thought her heart had been beating fast before, it felt like it might career right out of her chest now at the look of intent on his face. She took a deep breath, slid her feet into her shoes and took the hand he offered.

The band started playing a slow, lazy tune in deference to the late hour. Catching her fingers in his, Nico pulled her to him. One hand laced through his, the other resting on his shoulder, she moved into his arms. Shivered as he slid an arm around her waist and pulled her into an utterly respectable hold that somehow didn't feel so innocent with the undercurrents running between them.

His palm at her back burned like a brand against her bare skin. When she tipped her head back, there was a sexy, smoky heat in his eyes that turned her insides to mush.

"Are you sure you can handle this?" he murmured. "I don't do relationships, Chloe. If we do this, it's to burn this thing between us out. We both walk into it on the same page. Nobody gets hurt."

Her core melted into a pool of fire.

She pulled in a deep breath. Gathered her courage. "I know what I want," she said firmly. "I've always known what I want. If this past year has taught me anything, it's that life is short. You have to seize the moment. And I don't want to spend tonight alone. I want to spend it with you."

He fixed her with an unreadable gaze. Her chest felt tight, hot, as if she could hardly breathe. Finally, after an interminably long moment that seemed to stretch forever, he bent his head to her ear. "You have security access to my penthouse from the night you dropped those papers off. Finish up here and meet me there. I'll leave after you do."

CHAPTER TEN

NICO'S PENTHOUSE ON Fifth Avenue was dark and masculine, with a stunning cityscape view through floor-to-ceiling windows that left the entire space encased in glass.

Chloe kicked off her shoes in the foyer and walked into the open-concept living room with its jaw-dropping panorama of Manhattan. Oyster suede sofas and tan leather chairs were scattered around the space, gleaming birch floors a perfect foil for the dark architecture of the room. But she was too nervous to sit still, Mireille's analysis of Nico burned into her brain.

Nico isn't a forever kind of guy. He's a night-to-remember guy.

Her stomach swooped, like a book dropping off a high shelf. Was she crazy to think she could handle this? What if she couldn't? What if she was a disaster in bed with him—too nervous to enjoy any of it? She'd slept with only one man in her entire life, and that hadn't been a momentous experience.

She stood there, stomach crawling with nerves, until she heard the swish of the elevator arriving. The sound of Nico depositing his keys on the front table. She didn't turn around when he walked into the living room because she was too apprehensive to. The thud of his jacket hitting the sofa made her jump. Sent goose bumps to every inch of her skin as the sound of jazzy, sexy music filled the room.

Part of his practiced seduction routine? She almost jumped out of her skin when his hands settled around her waist and he pulled her back against him, his delicious dark, sensual scent wrapping itself around her.

"Maybe we should have a drink," she breathed. "I seem to be a bit jumpy."

"We don't need a drink," he said huskily. "I think we should dance instead. I didn't get a chance to do that with you. Not the way I wanted to."

She sucked in badly needed air. Closed her eyes as he bit down ever so gently on her earlobe, the sensual caress ricocheting through her. "How would that be?" she managed to croak.

He didn't answer. Turned her around and took her in his arms instead. The fingers of one hand laced through hers, he splayed the other across her hip. Possessive, intimate, it made her pulse pound.

His forehead resting against hers, they danced to the sultry tune. Their bodies in perfect sync, as if they'd been molded to fit together, it was, quite simply, the most heart-stoppingly romantic moment of her life.

"Nico," she murmured. And then his mouth was on hers, his thumb stroking her cheek, the slow, leisurely slide of their lips against each other like the magical prelude to a passionate symphony that would only build and grow.

She stood on tiptoe. Curved her fingers around his neck. Moved deeper into the kiss until she wasn't sure where she began and he ended. His fingers at her jaw, he angled her head to position her the way he wanted her. She opened her mouth to his command, was rewarded by the lazy, sensual slide of his tongue against hers. Deeper, *hot-*

ter the kiss went until every limb in her body melted, utterly supine against his.

He moved the hand he had at her hip down over her bottom. Cupped her in his palm and brought her closer until she felt the thick, hard evidence of his erection against her. Her knees went weak, threatened to give way, but his hand at her buttock held her easily. Kept her pressed against his impressive arousal, his physical strength vastly exciting to her.

So *this* was the kind of dance he'd been talking about. Her blood thundered in her veins, her heart battered up against her ribs, every inch of her skin pulsed to life. It was like she'd spent her entire adult existence waiting for him to touch her like this. She wanted to memorize every second for future reference.

"Tell me what you like," he rasped in her ear. "How you like it. How you *want* it."

"Like that," she gasped as he rotated his hips against her in a sultry movement that turned her insides to molten honey. "You feel so good, Nico."

He took her mouth in a hungry kiss that held no restraint. Raw, erotic, he made love to her mouth with the hot slide of his tongue until she whimpered and pressed closer. He angled her more intimately against him and let her feel every centimeter of the steely length that pressed against his trousers. Gave her more of that pleasure that had driven her crazy that night at the pool.

"Don't stop," she whispered, on a broken plea. But he did, bending to slide his arm beneath her knees to pick her up and carry her to the bedroom. Setting her down beside the bed in the minimalistic airy room with a spectacular view as its only decor, he moved behind her, set his fingers to the zipper of her dress and drew it down. His hands settling around her hips, he pushed the dress up and over her head, cool air caressing her skin as he tossed it in a pool of silk on the floor.

A wave of self-consciousness settled over her as he sat down on the bed and drew her to him. His fingers dealt with the clasp of her bra with an experience and dexterity that made her pulse pound. Off it went into the pile. And then she was naked in front of him except for the black lace panties that clung to her hips.

Standing in front of him, his gaze level with

her bare, aching breasts, she took in the hunger in his stormy gray eyes. "You are so gorgeous," he said roughly. "So perfect. I need to have you, Chloe."

Her insides fell apart. He tugged her the last step forward. Cupped her breasts in his hands. Kneaded them, weighed them. Brushed his thumbs over the straining, tender tips until she moaned and pushed closer, his caresses melting her limbs.

With a muttered imprecation, he dropped to his knees in front of her, his hands cupping her buttocks to bring her close. "Nico," she murmured, heart racing as she read his intention. "You can't do that." No man had ever touched her like that.

He looked up at her, eyes hot. "I've waited forever to have you like this. I want to kiss you. Touch you. *Let me.*"

His words took her apart. Annihilated the last of her defenses, what she'd said to Lashaunta that day filling her head.

When you let yourself be stripped down, naked, raw, because this was you and you couldn't be anything else but who you are.

It had always been like that with Nico. He had seen every part of her. This would be no different.

She relaxed beneath his hands. Let him part her thighs. He pressed his lips to the trembling skin of her abdomen in a hot, openmouthed kiss. Her muscles tightened as he moved his mouth down to the band of her panties. *Lower.* And then he was caressing her through the damp lace with his mouth, his tongue, his hands at her bottom holding her in place for his delectation.

She dug her fingers into his coarse dark hair. Whispered mindless words of pleasure, her knees jelly beneath her. Begged for more. He sank his fingers into her hips, turned her around and pushed her back on the bed. Sliding his fingers beneath her panties, he stripped them off.

Her heart nearly burst through her chest as he pulled her to the edge of the bed and spread her thighs wide with his big palms. Drank her in. And then he parted her most delicate flesh with his fingers, his gaze reverential.

"You're beautiful here, too," he murmured. "So pink. Wet. *Perfect.*"

She closed her eyes. Curled her fingers in the

bedspread. He set his mouth to her, hot and knowing, doing the same wicked things he'd done to her before, only this time there was nothing between her and the searing caress of his mouth, and it was so earth-shatteringly delicious she was lost.

He fluttered his tongue over the tight bundle of nerves at the heart of her. Told her how good she tasted in raw, uncensored words that inflamed her. She begged for more. Holding her hips tighter, he laved her, flicked at her with his tongue, the powerful lash of his caress almost too much to bear.

Her back arched off the bed. "Nico—*please.*"

He slid a palm beneath her hips and lifted her up. Slid a thick, masculine finger inside her in a slow, controlled movement that made her crazy. Gently, insistently, he caressed her with firm, even strokes. It felt so good, so *amazing*, she bit down hard on the inside of her cheek to prevent the cry that rose in her throat.

"You like that?" he murmured huskily, eyes on hers. "It makes you crazy, doesn't it?"

She nodded in helpless surrender. Moved into the sexy, sensual caresses he was administering with a tilt of her hips, because she knew how he could make her come apart with those skillful, amazing hands of his.

The pleasure built. She dug her nails into the bedding, gasping her pleasure, because she couldn't hold it in anymore.

"That's it, sweetheart," he said throatily. "Talk to me. That's so damn sexy."

He filled her with two fingers. Worked them in and out until she was arched like a bow, sobbing for release. Then he pressed a palm to her abdomen, wrapped his lips around the peak of her sex and tugged at her until he sent her flying into a sweet, hot release that radiated from the heart of her outward, until every inch of her was in flames.

Nico felt like someone had drugged him as he pushed to his feet, eyes on Chloe as she lay sprawled across his bed. Exactly as he'd imagined her. But oh, so much more jaw dropping in the flesh.

She was perfection with her taut, high breasts… the slim curve of her waist that flared out to hips that were deliciously feminine…the long legs, toned and magnificent, that he wanted wrapped around him while he took her long and slow and hard.

He swiped a hand over his jaw, heart pounding. He could still taste her in his mouth, how sweet she was. Could still feel how perfect she'd felt beneath his hands—like silk. He craved her so much, his lust so thick in his throat, he wasn't even sure how he wanted to take her. He only knew that now that he'd given in to the insanity, he was going to drown himself in it.

She opened her eyes. Set her shimmering brown gaze on his. He started unbuttoning his shirt. Yanked it off, buttons flying, when it didn't happen quickly enough. Her eyes darkened as he undid his pants, slid the zipper down and pushed them off his hips, his boxers following close behind. The heat of her gaze turned him hard as a rock.

He lifted a brow. "You didn't answer my question."

"About?" Her voice was lazy. Sated.

"How you want it?"

That woke her up. She levered herself up on

her elbows. Worried her lip with her teeth. "I don't know."

"What?" he gibed. "There's finally something you would like to defer to me on?"

"Yes." She sank her teeth deeper into the soft flesh he wanted to taste again. It tipped him over the edge.

"You on top," he said evenly. *"Now."*

Her eyes widened. He found a condom in the bedside table. Stretched himself out on the bed and beckoned to her. She crawled over to him, uncertainty and desire glittering in her beautiful eyes.

"You took on the world tonight," he murmured. "Surely you can handle me."

The uncertainty morphed into a look of pure challenge. She straddled him, her gorgeous body a feast for the eye. It was such a turn-on, this confident, spectacular creature she'd turned into, he was transfixed. High color streaking her cheeks, her hair a tumble of silk around her face, she bent to kiss him.

"You were saying?" she murmured, lips parting sweetly against his. He reached up, cupped the back of her head and brought her closer, his mouth melding with warm, honeyed temptation. She tasted exquisite, the subtle stroke of her tongue against his as she kissed him deeply, intimately, offering him all of her in that way she had that made him completely lose his head.

Her hands found his hard length pulsing against his thigh. She caressed him, her smooth, even strokes unpracticed and so much more hot because of it. He cursed as she pushed him close to the edge. "Baby," he murmured, clamping a hand around hers. "Either you do this or I take control."

Her eyes flashed. She didn't like that idea. He handed her the condom. Her hands stumbled over the task. He settled his fingers over hers and rolled it on, the intimate act thickening the air between them to unbearable levels.

Blood pounded his temples as she positioned herself over top of him. Brought the thick crest of his arousal to her slick velvet heat. Cradled against her, he rubbed the length of her. Relished her low groan.

"Nico."

It was his turn to groan as she took him just

barely inside her. "Slowly," he bit out. "*Dio*. You are so tight."

Her eyes locked on his as she took him deeper, the erotic connection between them so hot it fried his brain. He set his palm low on her belly. Found her center with the pad of his thumb and massaged her in slow, sensual circles. She closed her eyes, full mouth slackening. Her body softened, took him deeper inside, slowly, excruciatingly slowly, until finally she had sheathed him with her hot, silky flesh.

She opened her eyes. Fixed them on his. "I didn't know it could be like this," she breathed. "You feel so good, Nico."

Blood roared in his head. He could have told her it wasn't like this. Not usually. That sex could be good, but it wasn't always this mind-blowing. But that would be admitting things he chose to ignore. That she had always touched a piece of him no one else ever had.

He grasped her hips in his hands. Moved her against him in a slow circle. She was plush, tight, so damn good, he almost lost it right then and there. Gritting his teeth, he counted from ten back to one. Which proved ineffectual when, eyes trained on his, she picked up his rhythm. Drove him insane with the sexy, circular movements of her voluptuous hips.

He curved a hand around her nape. Brought her mouth down to his. Mated his tongue with hers as he possessed her hot, sweet body with insistent, powerful thrusts that made her gasp with every drive. She begged, panted into his mouth. Hands at her hips, he positioned her so she came down at the right angle for him to hit that tender spot inside her.

"Like that," she gasped. "Oh, Nico. Like that."

"Let go," he bit out, fighting a deep, primal need to take. To mark her as his as he'd always wanted to. Then lost the battle as her body contracted around his in a tight fist and she cried out, nails digging into his shoulders. His hands grasping her hips, he thrust up inside her, yanking her down to meet his punishing lunges.

Harder and thicker he swelled inside her, taking his pleasure, until she splintered him apart in a deep, shuddering release and he came harder than he ever had in his life.

The rasp of their breathing the only sound in the room, he held her, sprawled across his chest, stroking a hand over the silky, soft skin of her back until she fell into an exhausted sleep curled against him.

An insidious tendril of unease wound its way through him alongside the powerful, more potent emotions swamping him in the aftermath of the intimacy they'd shared.

It was just good sex, he told himself. Perhaps the best he'd ever had. He and Chloe shared an intense physical attraction—one he'd been fighting for far too long. What man wouldn't react that way when a woman was so sweet and willing in his arms? So sexy and vulnerable all at the same time?

Curving Chloe's soft, warm body against his, he let sleep take him. They were going to need some *rules*. But tomorrow would be soon enough to have those awkward, line-reinforcing kinds of conversations they needed to have.

CHAPTER ELEVEN

CHLOE WOKE TO the first, soft yellow light of day making its way into the sky, shrouding the tall skyscrapers in an almost otherworldly glow. It was such a magnificent view, she simply drank it in for a moment.

Her sensory perception expanded beyond the jaw-dropping panorama to the heavy, solid weight draped around her middle. The hot, hard male body pressed against the length of hers. The very *naked* hot, hard male body pressed against hers.

She was in Nico's bed. She'd spent the night with Nico. *OMG.*

Her heart thumped wildly in her chest. She pressed a palm to the hard, staccato beat in an attempt to steady its racing rhythm, but nothing seemed to help. Everything felt utterly off-kilter—like it would never be the same again. Not after *that*.

She sucked in a deep breath. Blew it out slowly.

Last night had been indescribable. Romantic. Sensual. *Soul consuming*. Everything she'd dreamed about and more.

She'd always known Nico would be an amazing lover. That unparalleled control of his, the intensity he wore like a glove, the sensuality that was so much a part of him. But nothing could have prepared her for the depth of intimacy they had shared. It made her toes curl to even think about it.

It seemed impossible to imagine that what they had shared was an ordinary connection. It felt *extraordinary*. Nico had taken her apart, exposed every part of her. Made her feel so alive it was *terrifying*. And she could have sworn he'd felt it, too. That it could be the start of something amazing if he let down his walls.

And maybe that was highly naive, unwise thinking. She had no experience with a man like Nico. With that kind of passion. Maybe what they'd shared was simply powerful chemistry. The only thing she *was* sure of was that she was completely and utterly out of her depth.

She sank her teeth into her lip. Twisted to face him. His arm fell away to rest above his head, his severe features relaxed, long dark lashes shading his cheeks. He was so gorgeous it made her melt. But it wasn't just the stunning outer packaging that drew her to him. It was the man *inside* the gorgeous facade. Who he was at the heart of him—impregnable in a storm, unyielding in his sense of honor, solid in a way she'd never encountered.

Finding out he was the man she'd always believed him to be had only underscored the feelings she'd always had for him. Made them more inevitable. If she was smart, she knew, she'd guard her heart. Keep her head.

She turned back to look at the bedside clock. *Six thirty. Thank goodness.* Some internal alarm must have woken her. She needed to be downtown at the Times Square store by 8:00 a.m. to prep for Lashaunta's appearance. Given she had no clothes, only the dress she'd worn the night before, that was a problem she needed to rectify. *Fast.*

She slid out of bed. Went searching for her underwear. Another wash of heat claimed her cheeks as she found it scattered around the room. Snatching up her bra and panties, she slid them and her dress on. Pursed her lips as she considered a sleeping Nico. Was she supposed to wake him up and say goodbye? What *was* the proper procedure?

In the end, she let him sleep. Maybe it was the coward in her, because she wasn't sure how to handle this right now. But it seemed the easier way.

Facing Nico's elegant, perfectly pressed doorman while clad in her sparkly dress and high heels wasn't so easy. What did Mireille call it? The *walk of shame*? It certainly felt like it. The doorman, however, greeted her smoothly and whistled for a taxi, as if seeing off women dressed for the night before was all part of a day's work. A good reminder that she was simply *one* of those women for Nico.

She showered and changed at home, then jetted downtown. The crowds outside the store stretched for blocks, Lashaunta every bit the draw she'd hoped she would be. Practically jumping up and down with excitement, Chloe watched as the pop singer sang four songs from her new album for the crowd and the shelves began to empty of the limited-edition Be. Her problem, she soon realized, was going to be keeping up with the demand, because the same thing was happening worldwide.

She was practically floating on air by the time she arrived back at the office. She had just enough time to check in with Clara before she sailed into a meeting. Which was a budget meeting that happened to include Nico. The nerves came back like a fast-moving tornado.

Sitting across from her at the large boardroom table full of executives, he looked ridiculously handsome in a dark, pin-striped suit and a crisp white shirt. Her heart tripped over itself as she took a sip of the coffee Clara had thankfully provided. He had one of those inscrutable looks on his face. All business.

She told herself to play it cool. Wrapped her nerves in a reservoir of calm she wasn't close to feeling. But she couldn't concentrate on the meeting for the life of her. She kept wondering where she and Nico stood after last night.

After an hour of attempting to pretend he didn't exist, she weakened near the end of the meeting and allowed herself a glance at him. Found him staring at her, a flash of something in his gray eyes that made her breath catch in her throat.

"Nico?" the CFO prompted. "You on board with that?"

Nico nodded.

"Chloe?"

She stared blindly at the balding executive. "Ah—yes. Definitely."

"Good. Let's move on."

Nico was in a bit of a mood. He had never, in his life, had a woman walk out on him after a night spent together. There was an etiquette to it—an acknowledgment of how good it had been—a mutual expression of *appreciation* to be communicated.

Instead, he'd woken to an empty bed. Not a text, not a note. He'd known Chloe had her event today, had planned to drive her home *after* he'd had her again this morning. And perhaps that was the problem. He'd woken up hard and hungry for her with a need that hadn't abated, and that was never a good way to start the morning.

He sat back in his chair. Took a slug of his coffee. Considered her across the table. Just to be clear, it *had* been mind-bendingly good sex. *Emotional* sex, even. The most intensely involved experience of his life, if he were to be honest. They had been crazy for each other. So where was the clinginess every woman seemed to display the morning after? It didn't seem to be coming. Instead, Chloe looked cool and aloof. Distant. *Did she regret last night?*

The meeting drew to a close. Chloe headed for the door. Nico moved fast, stepping into the hallway at the same time she did.

"A minute," he said softly.

Simone, who'd left the room behind them, stopped to ask him something. Her gaze shifted from Nico to Chloe and back again. Registered the charge in the air. She murmured something about asking him the question later and moved off in the direction of his office.

Nico looked at Chloe. "How did the launch go?"

She leaned back against the wall, eyes on his, her lip caught between her teeth. "It went great. We sold out. Had to restock."

"Congratulations." He leaned a palm on the door frame beside her, catching a whiff of her elusive, sexy perfume. "Do you have any idea what budget you just agreed to in there?"

She shook her head. "None."

"You don't think that's a bit irresponsible?"

"I do." A slow nod. "Forgive me. My mind was elsewhere."

"*Where*, exactly?"

"The regions," she murmured. "I have a call with Europe in minutes."

A curl of heat unleashed itself inside him. He didn't believe her for a minute. But he had a meeting, too. "We can talk later, then."

"Of course."

It wasn't until seven o'clock that evening, however, that he had a chance to seek Chloe out, a brutal day of meetings behind him. She was in her office sitting behind her desk, frowning over a report of some kind. Her suit jacket discarded on the back of her chair, she looked gorgeous in a sheer cream silk blouse and a gray pencil skirt that showed off her fabulous legs.

He wanted to unbutton her and consume her whole. But first, he wanted to find out what was wrong with her.

Wary, so wary, were the big brown eyes that

landed on his as he shut the door behind him. But there was also a shimmering, dark glitter in her gaze, a sensual awareness that heated his skin.

He walked over to lean against her desk. "What's going on? And don't tell me it's Vivre, because I'm not buying it for a second. I've seen the sales reports. They're astounding."

She put down her pen. "Nothing's going on. What do you mean?"

Frustration fizzled up his spine. "Okay," he murmured, "let's talk about last night, then. How are you feeling about it? Usually women like to talk about it. I thought you might want to, since you walked out this morning without a word."

A guarded look crossed her face. "I had to get to my event. I didn't want to wake you."

"I was going to *drive* you there, had you woken me up. You took a damn taxi home, Chloe. That is not all right."

Her lashes lowered, sweeping her cheeks like miniature black fans. "Last night was amazing, Nico. More than I ever could have imagined. I don't regret a thing, if that's what you're wondering."

Straightforward, matter-of-fact. *Honest.* But

then again, this was Chloe, and she didn't play games like other women. She wasn't *like* any other woman he'd ever met. Hadn't he always known that? Wasn't that what had scared him away in the first place? Everything he wanted to know was right there on her face. In those ebony eyes, which looked terribly uncertain at the moment.

"If that's the case," he said quietly, "then why do you look like that?"

"Like what?"

"Like you regret it."

"I don't regret it."

"Chloe," he growled.

She closed her eyes. Was silent for a long moment before she opened them again. "I am out of my depth," she said softly. "You took me apart last night, Nico. Split me wide-open. It *affected* me. *You* affect me. I was trying to get my equilibrium back."

The muscles around his heart contracted. He'd known this was going to happen. Known it was going to be a mess. Chloe had never been able to separate her emotions from her head. But neither could he lie to himself and pretend last night had been just about sex, because it hadn't. What he felt for her had always been more complex than that.

"You don't think I feel something for you?" he rasped, eyes on the naked vulnerability written across her face. "You don't think I was *affected* by last night? You don't think I'm crazy for you, Chloe? Examine my behavior over the past few weeks and it might give you a clue."

She stared at him. The muscles in her throat convulsed. "I want to kiss you again," she whispered. "So badly, I can't stop thinking about it."

His blood fired. Pushing her chair back with a foot, he sank his hands into her waist and lifted her onto the desk in a single, fluid movement that pulled a gasp from her throat. "You should get on that," he said softly, planting his hands on the wood on each side of her thighs. "Although," he murmured, lowering his head to hers so their breath mingled in a warm, intimate caress, "I'm not sure just a kiss is what I'm looking for."

Her breath hitched. He waited, until she curved her fingers around his nape and brought him the rest of the way. It was all he needed to take her mouth in a hot, greedy kiss that blew his brains out. Cupping his jaw in her palms, she kissed him back, opening her mouth for him as he stroked inside with his tongue. Arched her neck back to take him deep.

He abandoned her mouth to explore the delicate line of her jaw. Traced the throbbing line of her pulse with his tongue. His hands dealt with the pearl buttons on her blouse with ruthless efficiency. Exposed her beautiful, rose-tipped breasts cupped in cream lace.

"Nico," she murmured huskily. "We are in the office."

"Everyone's gone home. I checked."

One hand on her hip, the other closed around her breast, he bent and licked the tip of one tightly furled nipple. Absorbed the low moan that raked through her. Played her, teased her, until she pushed into his hand and demanded more. Cupping her firmly, he took her deep into the heat of his mouth. Rolled the straining, taut nub over his tongue. Between his teeth. She was so lush and perfect, so responsive to his touch, she lit his blood on fire.

He transferred his attention to her other nipple. Swirled his tongue around the hard peak as he plumped her other breast in his palm. "I need to have you," he whispered against her ear.

Dragging her closer with the hand he held at her hip, he pushed her skirt up her thighs until he exposed her cream lace panties. They were so sexy against her coffee-colored skin, the blood thundered in his veins.

"Nico," she breathed. "We can't do this here."

"Yes, we can." He stepped between her thighs. Cupped her knee. Gentled her mouth with his. "Let me touch you, please you," he murmured against her mouth. "I need to have you."

Her knees fell apart. She watched him with big, hot eyes as he cupped her damp warmth with his palm. Inhaled the musky smell of her desire. "*Dio*, what you do to me," he breathed. "You make me lose my mind."

Pulling her panties aside, he ran a finger down her desire-swollen folds. Caressed her with lei-surely strokes. Her eyes darkened to twin ebony pools.

"Nico," she breathed.

He circled his finger at the slick entrance to her body. Pushed in gentle demand. She was silky and exquisitely tight. He eased inside her, waited while she adjusted to his touch.

"Please." She fixed her gaze on his.

He moved his finger in and out of her in a slow, sweet rhythm that had her moving to meet him with greedy movements of her hips. Pressing a kiss to the ultra-sensitive skin below her ear, he filled her again and again. Felt the tiny tremors that moved through her.

"Nico." She pressed against him in a sinuous movement.

He set his lips to her temple. "You want to come for me, baby?"

"Please."

He rubbed his thumb against her while he filled her with two fingers. Parted them inside her to caress her intimately. To ready her for his possession because he was like steel beneath his pants and she was small and delicate and he wanted her with a craving he'd never felt before—a voracious need that threatened to consume him.

"Nico," she begged, sinking her fingernails into his shoulders.

Wild for her, utterly unhinged, he reached for the button of his trousers, undid it and pushed his zipper down. Pulling her to the edge of the desk, he slid one hand beneath her hip, palmed his hard, hot flesh with the other and slotted himself against her velvet heat. The sensation of her silken flesh cradling him was indescribable.

He let out an oath. Chloe pulled back to look at him.

"A condom," he gritted out.

"I'm protected," she murmured. "It's fine."

He pushed inside, her tissues like liquid fire around him—squeezing him, stroking his length. His mouth at her ear, he told her how much she affected him, how much he wanted her, how much he'd *always* wanted her. She arched her hips, took him deep, until he was buried to the hilt. Seated inside her, sharing the ultimate intimacy, he held her gaze as he withdrew completely, then pushed back in, a mind-blowing, staggering penetration that made his heart beat like a drum.

"Nico." Her passion-filled gaze rested on his, dark, luminous, *irresistible*.

"You make me break all my rules," he rasped. "Every damn one."

He took her mouth in a hot, hungry kiss. Knew

in that moment that one more taste of her had been his undoing. That now that he'd let himself have her, he wouldn't be able to stop. But he was too far gone to care.

Grasping her hips tighter, he thrust inside her with a power that made her gasp, until they came together in a release that shook him to his core.

CHAPTER TWELVE

CHLOE WAS SO EXCITED, she could hardly contain herself.

Checking her appearance in the mirror for what might have been the fifth time, she convinced herself her short fiery-red dress, made of some rich, satiny material that showed a different depth of color every time she moved, was not, in fact, too short, her makeup—subtle but smoky—was unsmudged and the sleek hairstyle she'd chosen to match the sophisticated dress still in place.

She looked the same as she had five minutes ago. But maybe the dress *was* too short.

Oh, for heaven's sake. She spun away from the mirror with a disgusted sound and rummaged for her evening bag in the drawer. Perhaps it was the leftover adrenaline from the Soar launch with Eddie today that was making her jumpy. It had been amazing, frenetic, every TV camera in town out for it. Or maybe, she conceded, stomach clenching with nerves, it was the fact that Nico was back from Europe tonight, she hadn't seen him for a week and he was escorting her to Eddie's *Score* movie premiere.

She shoved a lip gloss and her phone into her bag, along with her keys. It could also have been the very sexy phone conversation she and Nico had shared last night when he'd gotten back to his hotel room that had left her skin crawling with anticipation. Or the way they'd gorged on each other for the two weeks before he'd left, Nico seeking her out in the lab or in her office each night, as if he couldn't resist the pull between them any more than she could.

She was falling for him—truly, madly, deeply—an unchecked spiral she knew wasn't wise. If she were *smart*, she acknowledged, pulling high black heels from her closet, she would be keeping her emotions out of this. Sticking to the deal she'd made with Nico, with *herself*, of a no-strings-attached fling. But she was sure he felt something more for her, too. Something deeper. Felt it every time he touched her. She thought he was hiding behind his walls—that it was going to take him time to trust how he felt.

And maybe, she conceded, sliding the heels on, that was simply the rosy view she chose to paint for herself. Maybe it had nothing to do with reality.

And maybe, she concluded, stomach sliding out from beneath her, she needed to get her head together. That appeared to be a top priority.

Snatching up her bag, she went downstairs and pulled a warm wrap from the closet. Was digging through her bag to make sure she'd thrown in the right lip gloss to match the vibrant dress when the doorbell rang.

Her heart beat a jagged rhythm. Setting the bag on the entryway table, she rubbed damp palms against her thighs and pulled in a steadying breath. Attempted to manage some sort of composure as she undid the two dead bolts her father had installed on the door.

All of it, unfortunately, flew out of her head as she swung the door open to find Nico leaning against the brick wall of the entrance in black jeans, a white shirt and a blazer.

God, she loved him in jeans. There wasn't a man on the planet who looked better in denim, all long legs, lean hips and raw masculinity. And then there were the muscles bulging beneath the hip tailored jacket—those powerful, corded arms she'd learned he needed only one of which to hold her in extremely creative positions.

Good heavens, Chloe. She dragged her gaze up to his. Registered the amusement glittering in his gray eyes.

"Hold that thought," he murmured. "Unless you'd like to skip the movie. I'm more than up for that."

Her stomach did a flip at that very tempting idea. But she shook her head with a smile. "Not a chance."

She'd never attended a premiere before, and this one was slated to be extremely glamorous with Hollywood's biggest stars set to shine. Not to mention the fact that Soar was going to be everywhere: in the Evolution refreshing stations at the after-party, in the gift bags for attendees, not to mention the fact that Eddie would be wearing it. She didn't plan on missing a minute.

"Bene." He walked past her into the hallway and shut the door. She turned to face him, heart thumping like a drum. Snaking an arm around her waist, he tugged her to him, one hand land-

ing on her hip, the other at her jaw. Nudging her up on tiptoes with the hand he held at her bottom, he brought his head down to hers.

"I *like* this," he murmured, sliding a hand over her silk-covered bottom. "It's very sexy. I'm going to enjoy taking it off you."

She couldn't answer because she was pretty much panting for him to kiss her, the brush of his lips against hers igniting a thousand tiny lightning strikes in her blood. Then he did, claiming her mouth in a deep, slow kiss that melted her bones, a sensual tasting that seemed to last a lifetime. Powerless to resist, she wound her arms around his neck and surrendered.

She felt his smile against her mouth as he ended the kiss oh-so-languidly and let her feet slide to the ground. When she might have slithered right to the floor, he held her up with the hand he had at her bottom.

"That was wholly unfair," she whispered, eyes on his.

"Say the word and we stay in."

She pressed a kiss to the hard line of his mouth. "Hold that thought."

He gave her a look that said he'd rather not.

Chloe's mouth curved in a smile as he escorted her to his car and spirited them the short distance to the Museum of Modern Art in midtown Manhattan, where the premiere was being held.

The red carpet shimmered in the spotlight as they arrived at the entrance to the impressive modern building, its entire exterior facade a wall of gleaming glass. The crowd that had gathered to watch the arrival of the stars was dozens deep.

They wouldn't walk the carpet, only the stars would, but Chloe wanted to watch, so they joined Santo and his date in a viewing area for guests off to the side, the atmosphere in the crowd electric. Santo didn't blink an eye at the protective hand Nico had placed at her back, introducing his date instead, a lovely reporter for one of the New York dailies. And then the stars were arriving in long black limousines.

Near the end of the parade of Hollywood glamour came Eddie and his sultry, stunning girlfriend, actress Camille Hayes. Tall and sleek in a plunging silver-and-gold gown, Camille was outrageously beautiful, the perfect dark foil for Eddie's blond good looks. His hand at her back, he escorted her down the red carpet to the appreciative roars of the crowd.

Chloe was so thrilled, she could hardly stand it. Eddie had a megawatt star power that glittered like no other with his saucy smile and entertaining wit as he talked to the press. And with her Soar ad playing on a screen just to the right of the logo-emblazoned step and repeat banner where the stars stopped for photographs, Evolution was front and center tonight.

If she could get any higher, Chloe thought, as they moved inside to watch the action-packed adventure movie *Score*, she wasn't sure how. It was the most exciting night of her life.

The after-party for *Score* was held in a trendy, swish bar close to the museum. A New York institution, the establishment was legendary for its elaborate Christmas decorations, draped in fifty thousand dollars' worth of glitz tonight, according to Santo, who kept track of such useless trivia.

Nico immediately felt his skin tighten at the overabundance of shiny balls, icicles and endless lights hung from every available surface. He would have turned around and walked out the door if it had been any other occasion. But Chloe was having fun, and far be it for him to steal her joy when she'd worked so hard for her achievements. When Evolution was shining tonight and Eddie Carello had taken it upon himself to introduce her around as the creator of his signature fragrance, his massive ego out in full force.

Ignoring the whole unavoidable ambience, he caught up with his brothers at the bar, while Chloe took Mireille and Santo's date off to visit the Vivre refreshment bar, where patrons could touch up their makeup and perfume.

"No date?" Nico observed as Lazzero did his usual aloof, unattainable routine leaning against the bar, which only made half the women in the room turn and stare.

Lazzero lifted a shoulder, his eyes trained on a group of people near the windows. "I felt like flying solo."

Nico followed his brother's perusal to a beautiful brunette who stood at the edge of the group. "Who is she?"

"Who?" His brother took a sip of his bourbon.

"The woman you keep staring at."

"No one important." Lazzero dismissed the subject, clearly unwilling to discuss the fact that she was *something*, because he'd undoubtedly had about twenty women lined up to accompany him this evening and he'd chosen to come alone. But Nico had learned a long time ago Lazzero confided when and how he wanted to.

Santo pointed his glass of bourbon at Nico, clearly coming to the same conclusion. "I see *you're* keeping better company these days."

Nico kept his tone nonchalant. "Chloe and I have agreed on a casual thing."

Santo took a sip of his bourbon. Rolled it around his mouth as he considered him. "You don't just casually see a woman like Chloe. You do it with intent or you don't do it at all."

Nico, who'd been ignoring that very fact for weeks, inclined his head. "And your point is?"

"Nothing," Santo said innocently. "I was just making an observation."

An observation that once in Nico's head, refused to budge as a friend of Santo's came up to greet them and Lazzero set off in the direction of the brunette. His head half in the conversation and half out, he considered Chloe in the very sexy red dress as she chatted up an A-list actress at the perfume bar.

She was glowing, in her glory tonight. It did something strange to his insides to see her like this, rearranged them in a foreign pattern he didn't recognize. She was smart, beautiful, passionate and empathetic. *Transparent.* Everything he'd convinced himself didn't exist in a woman.

He *had* missed her while he'd been in Europe, and not just in a physical sense. He'd missed her *presence.* How alive she made him feel. How she filled him up in places he hadn't even known he'd been empty.

He was crazy about her, if the truth be told.

The admission, after weeks of denial, rocked him back on his heels. But then again, he conceded, taking a sip of his bourbon, hadn't he subconsciously known it was true? He'd broken every one of his rules for her. Was *still* breaking them. And it felt right in a way he couldn't articulate.

"Can you believe it?" Chloe said, bubbling over with excitement as she rejoined him, champagne glass in hand, and they walked outside to the patio to get some fresh air. "Sasha Pierce wants me to design a custom perfume for her. *Sasha Pierce*, Nico. She's *legendary*."

He smiled, drawing her back against his chest as they stood at the railing and enjoyed a view of a light-emblazoned Manhattan. "Of course she wants you to design a perfume for her. Be is the number three fragrance in the world right now. Soar is going to be a huge hit. You're the talk of the town."

She wrinkled her nose. "Not quite."

She was silent for a moment, as if taking it all in, the silence of the high balcony wrapping itself around them. The balcony was deserted, the heaters not quite able to keep up with the chill in the air. And for that Nico was glad because it gave him a chance to clear his head.

Chloe swiveled to look up at him. "Are you having fun, though? You seem quiet."

He shrugged. "It isn't really my thing. But you're having fun—that's what matters."

Something in Nico's voice, a quiet, distant note, made Chloe lean back against the railing to look up at him. Study his face in the diffused, soft lighting the lamps cast across them. "What's wrong?" she murmured. "You've been off since we arrived."

Another of those uncommunicative shrugs. "It's nothing. Jet lag."

"Nico," she said softly, trailing a finger down his cheek. "I know you well enough now to know something's wrong."

"My mother walked out on New Year's Day," he said flatly. "A week later our house was re-possessed by the bank. This time of year doesn't hold very good memories for me."

Her throat locked, her skin stretching pain-fully tight across her body. "I'm so sorry. I didn't know. You never said anything."

"It wasn't exactly dinner-table conversation at the house in Great Neck."

She considered the hard, impenetrable lines of his face. "That must have been awful."

"It was surreal." A shadow whispered across the clarity of his gaze. "My father lost it that day. I mean actually *lost* it. He had been sinking into a depression for some time, but when she walked out, it was the end of him."

A knot formed in her throat. Grew until it was hard to swallow. He'd been only *fifteen*.

"What did you do? Where did you go?"

He balanced his glass on the railing. "I called my basketball coach. He was a mentor to me and my brothers. He knew a guy who owned a corner store in the neighborhood. I went to work for him, and he let us live in the apartment above the store in exchange for the work."

While he'd gone to school at night, refusing to give up on his own future. Her heart gave a painful lurch. "Lazzero and Santo were so young," she murmured. "They must have been devastated."

His mouth flattened. "They were in shock. Lazzero retreated into himself, refused to talk. Typical him. Santo started to cry because he wasn't sure which bike to take with him."

The ache inside her deepened until it hurt to breathe. She bit the inside of her mouth, the salt tang of blood staining her senses. "I think," she said huskily, reaching up to smooth her fingers over the hard line of his jaw, "that you are extraordinary, Nico Di Fiore. That you had the composure and presence of mind to take charge at that age."

He lifted a shoulder. "Who else was going to

do it? It wasn't easy—no. I was bitter. Angry at the responsibility I hadn't asked for. Angry at my *life* and the loss of my freedom. But you do what you have to do."

Worse, she imagined, was what it would have been like to watch the man he'd so clearly admired in his father suffer from such a debilitating disease. To become a shadow of himself.

She tipped her head to the side. "You said in Palm Beach you think of your father as the man he was, not the man he became. What was he like—in the early days?"

"Complex." He took a sip of the bourbon. Swirled it around the glass. "He was never home when we were young. The life of an investment banker—always on, always working, always socializing with clients. It made my mother crazy. But to me," he acknowledged with a faint smile, "he was larger than life. He loved us, loved being a father. Whenever he did have time to spend with us, it was the best. He would take us to baseball games, up to the cottage, out fishing. That's when he was his true self. Away from all the pressure."

She frowned. "I remember my father saying

he was *the guy* on Wall Street. That everybody wanted to be him. That he was fueled by this ambition that seemed to consume him." She pressed the rim of her glass to her chin. "Where did that come from, do you think?"

He considered the question for a moment before replying. "The estrangement from his own father was a part of it. His father was abusive to his mother. He tried so many times to intercede—to persuade his mother to leave—but she wouldn't. So he left when he couldn't handle it anymore and came to New York to start a life for himself. He had nothing. No money, no one to fall back on. *He* was it.

"It fueled his ambition on Wall Street. He was imminently successful because of it—a risky, brilliant deal maker. But his ambition was also his Achilles' heel. Once he got caught up in the rush, he couldn't turn it off. He constantly needed *more*. The money, the power—it all went to his head. He had affairs, began living on the razor's edge."

Chloe frowned. "So your mother had reasons for being unhappy, other than the loss of her career?"

Antagonism darkened his gaze. "She *drove* him to it. She was never happy, not from the beginning. The affairs weren't right, clearly, but I can see why it happened."

And she could see the whole story was far more complex than it seemed on the surface, even if she understood why Nico wanted to blame his mother for all of it. "There are always two sides to a story," she said, treading carefully. "Perhaps you don't know the whole truth."

His jaw hardened. "Perhaps I don't want to know. Perhaps I don't care. Maybe it's a fact that two people always mess up a relationship one way or another."

"That's not true," she countered quietly. "Look at my parents. How in love they were. What a great team they were. They were *stronger* together."

"What Martino and Juliette had is a rarity, I promise you."

"Perhaps," she agreed. "But it does exist."

"Anything's possible." He shook his head at her. "Don't start spinning romantic illusions around me, Chloe. I've never been a believer in fairy tales. My experiences have taught me differently."

She took a sip of her champagne. Studied the cynicism on his face. He made so much sense to her now—why he was the way he was. He had the same driving ambition his father had had, for exactly the same reasons. Because his once-safe, if tumultuous life had splintered apart and he would never let the same thing happen to him. Would never make the same mistakes his father had.

Instead, he had made himself into a rock in the middle of the storm for his brothers. For *her.* He had given Santo and Lazzero the faith that life could be trusted, people could be trusted, because he had *been there* for them like his parents hadn't been for him.

A hand fisted her insides. She wanted to be that for him. The one who taught Nico he could trust. That he could *believe* in what they had. Because she couldn't lie to herself any longer and say she didn't want all of him, because she did. She always had. And maybe, just maybe, she had enough faith for both of them.

Or perhaps, she acknowledged, her stomach hollowing out, she was setting herself up for a fall.

A dark fire lit his gaze. "Hey," he murmured, his arm sliding around her waist to pull her close. "That's ancient history. We are not letting it kill the mood. And I am in the *mood*. It's been a week since I've had you."

Heat shimmered through her insides. She let him remove her champagne glass from her hand. Framed his face with her hands as she kissed him long and deep. Refused to let fear rule her, that instinctive need to retreat that had always directed her actions, because she was through doing that. She was seeing this thing with Nico through to the end, just like she'd promised herself, because she thought he was worth it. She thought *they* were worth it.

"Are you ready to go?" he murmured, when they came up for air. "I'm done with *holding that thought*."

Her blood on fire for him, she nodded. They said their goodbyes to Mireille and his brothers, collected the car from the valet and made the drive back to Nico's penthouse in an expectant silence that had every nerve in her body tense with anticipation.

* * *

Nico tossed his keys on the entrance table when they walked into the penthouse, shrugged out of his jacket and threw it on a chair in the living room. Sinking his fingers into the knot of his tie, he set his gaze on Chloe as he stripped it off, his body hard and hungry after a week without her.

Lowering himself onto the sofa, he reached for her, pulled her onto his lap.

When her lush lips parted in invitation, her dark eyes full of passion, he didn't hesitate, didn't even try to resist her. Cupping her cheeks with his palms, he settled his mouth over hers in a hot, hungry kiss.

She sighed. He took full advantage, sliding his tongue inside her mouth to tangle with hers, tilting her jaw up to provide him with better access. The taste of her exploded through him, sweet from the champagne she'd consumed. Uniquely her.

He slid his hands beneath the slippery, shimmery material of her dress that had been inflaming him all evening. Found the warmth between her thighs and stroked her through the silky material of her panties with leisurely, teasing caresses. She moaned low in her throat, her soft, breathy sighs making him crazy. But when he would have lifted her to straddle him, desperate to have her, she swept her delicate hand along the hard ridge of him instead, erasing any coherent thought.

"Chloe," he murmured. "I am more than ready."

She ignored him, sliding her fingers up to the button of his jeans to undo it. Every muscle in his body tensed as she lowered his zipper, the rasp of metal against teeth amplifying the pounding of the blood in his head. And then her hands were on him, uncovering him, pulling him out of his boxers.

His heart thundered in his chest as she slid to the floor in front of him. She had been too shy to do that to him up until now, and he hadn't been into pushing her because he'd known with the passion they shared it would happen. He just wasn't sure he could handle it tonight. Didn't know if he had that in him with the need driving him.

He watched, transfixed, as she slid her mouth over the velvet length of him, used her lips and tongue to make him wild for her. Blood pulsing through his body, he arched into her touch, spellbound by her unpracticed seduction.

"Like this," he instructed hoarsely, sliding his hands over hers, showing her how he liked to be touched. How hard. How fast. How to drive him higher.

When he couldn't take it anymore, when he knew he'd finish it that way if he didn't put a stop to it, he reached for her, picked her up and laid her on the sofa like a feast for his consumption.

Red silk dress askew, plunging open to reveal her taut, creamy flesh, her long legs a tangle of olive skin, he had never known such lust. Such need. She was sweetness and innocence, brilliance and fire, an intoxication to his senses he couldn't seem to fight.

He pushed the dress up to her waist. The tiny panties that clung to her hips did little to hide the shadow of her femininity, firing his blood to a fever pitch. He spread his palm over her abdomen, absorbing the shiver that went through her. Trailed his fingers down to the tantalizing piece of silk that covered her. Eyes a deep, dark espresso, she watched him strip it from her.

He got rid of his pants and boxers in one swift

move. Came back over her, caging her in with his arms braced on each side of her. "You burn me up," he whispered against her mouth, "until I can't think for wanting you."

She pulled his head down to hers, her fingers sliding into his hair. He slicked his tongue over her lips and gained entry to her sweet mouth. Every stroke, every lick, sensual and earthy, bound him to her in a way he'd never experienced before.

Sliding his palm over her thigh, he found the hollow at the back of her knee. Curved her elegant leg around his waist so that she was open to him. His to take. Settling himself against her moist, welcome heat, he held her gaze as he stroked inside her with a single hard thrust. Claimed her tight, silken flesh with a possession that made her internal muscles spasm in erotic response.

"Fast or slow," he murmured. "Your choice."

"Slow," she breathed, eyes locked on his. "As slow as you can make it."

He regretted asking because he wasn't sure how slow he could take it. His breath coming hard and fast, he possessed her with smooth rhythmic strokes, corralling the fire raging through him as her silken body clenched around his pulsing flesh. Her eyes were liquid fire, the perfection they created together written across them as she curved her leg tighter around his waist and met him thrust for thrust.

It was too intense, *too much*. Burying his mouth in her neck, he tasted her salty skin as he drove harder into her amazing body until they came together in a rush of violent heat that blanked his head.

Emerging from a sex-induced haze what felt like hours later, he took her to bed and made love to her again. When he couldn't sleep, his internal clock messed up from the travel, or perhaps from the intensity of the emotion chasing through him, he left Chloe curled up in bed, went into the living room and poured himself a glass of water.

He carried it into the living room. Sat staring at an always-on Manhattan spread out before him.

He'd told himself he was walking into this thing with Chloe to burn out the attraction between them, when in reality what he'd really wanted was *her*. A no-strings-attached affair had been a convenient excuse to avoid admitting how he really felt about her. That she'd always made him want more. Made him want to *be* more, and he wasn't sure he could be that.

He cared about Chloe—deeply if he were to be honest. But even if he'd always suspected she might be *the one*, offering her the love she needed wasn't a place he was ever going to let himself go. He'd severed that piece of himself the day his life as he'd known it had imploded. Had told himself he needed no one because he'd had to— it was the only way he'd known how to exist.

He took a sip of the water. Tipped his head back as the cool liquid slid down his throat. What would happen when Chloe began to hate him for what he couldn't give her? Because it *would* happen eventually. People changed, emotions changed, and that was when it all fell apart. He knew it as surely as the sun would rise tomorrow.

Martino's voice from that Fourth of July night floated through his head, his raspy Italian lilt as clear as if it had been yesterday.

You need to make a choice, Nico. Decide whether you can give her what she needs or walk away.

Hearing the words now, filtered through a decade's worth of perspective, gave them a different cast. He had assumed Martino had been telling him to walk away, when what he realized now he'd been telling him was that he had a choice—he could decide he could be more, or he could remain the closed-off, hardened man he'd become.

Life was about choices.

How would he even know if he was capable of being what Chloe needed if he didn't try? Would he forgive himself if he didn't and let her go, only for some other man to offer her what he couldn't? He didn't think he would. Not now.

He sat there for a long time, his head too full to think. The only thing he was sure of was that Santo had been right. Either he committed to Chloe or he walked away. There was no in between.

Bright sunlight filtering through a crack in the blinds woke Chloe. She was alone in bed, the sound of water running in the en suite bathroom indicating Nico had risen before her. The man didn't sleep, she marveled, sinking back into the pillows to recall the utterly perfect evening of the night before.

She'd had so much fun showing off Vivre to

Hollywood. *A custom perfume for an A-list actress.* It was a coup worthy of her mother. Topped off by an utterly unforgettable, passionate night with Nico.

Her good mood persisted as she slid out of bed, intent on joining him in the shower because that was the way she liked best to wake up. She was almost across the room when her phone rang. *Mireille*, from the distinctive ringtone she reserved exclusively for her sister.

She frowned. Mireille was decidedly *not* a morning person. Maybe she'd seen all the social media coverage from last night and had called to congratulate her on a successful evening. Backtracking, she plucked the phone off the nightstand and took the call. "You're up early."

"Chloe." Her sister's voice was eerily calm. "You and Nico need to meet my team at the office as soon as you can get in."

Her fingers tightened around the phone. "Why?"

"Eddie got into a fight with Camille last night. A big blowup at Gianni's. Club security had to intervene. Also," her sister added, a grim note to her voice, "he said some very derogatory things about women someone caught on video. It's all over the internet."

Nooo. Cold fingers clamped down on her spine. The entire Vivre campaign was built around the empowerment of women.

"How bad is it?"

"Bad, Chloe. You need to get in here."

She sucked in air, her breath a sharp blade in her chest. Exhaled. Panic was not going to help. "We'll be there in thirty minutes."

Nico walked out of the bathroom, his brow furrowed. "What was that?"

She pushed a chunk of hair out of her face. Took another deep breath, but it seemed impossible to get the words out of her mouth. Because Nico had warned her about Eddie. He had wanted to cut him. And now, a week before Christmas, the most important sales week of the year, they had a disaster on their hands.

Nico tossed the shirt he was carrying on the bed, walked over to her and tipped her chin up with his fingers. "What's going on?"

She swallowed past the tightness constricting her throat. "It's Eddie. He went off the rails again last night. There was a fight with Camille at Gianni's...club security had to intervene. He also," she added, her gaze falling away from his, "said some awful things about women someone caught on video. It's all over the internet."

Nico uttered a filthy word she'd never heard him use before, his hands falling away from her face. Heart slamming against her ribs, she risked a look up at him, but he wasn't looking at her. He was in full damage-control mode.

"Get dressed," he said curtly. "Was that Mireille on the phone?"

"Yes." Her voice steadied in the face of his fury. "They're waiting for us at the office."

"Good." He ripped the towel off his hips and started to dress. She stood there, frozen.

"Nico, I'm sorry. This is— This *was* my fault."

He spared her a quick glance. "It doesn't matter whose fault it is. We need to fix it."

Mireille and the PR team were waiting in Nico's office when he and Chloe arrived thirty minutes later.

Mireille, always cool and composed, was ashen-faced. "I'm sorry. This was my call."

Nico waved the apology off. "It was a collective

decision. I could have cut him." Pouring himself a cup of coffee, he took a seat at the conference table, a move Chloe mimicked. "What's the game plan?"

Cara Cioni, Mireille's boss, who had two decades of experience managing crises for a major auto manufacturer, got up and went to the whiteboard. "First," she said, "we cut Eddie loose. Void the contract using the morality clause. But," she added, a frown pulling at her brow, "we have to be very careful with this. He's the most powerful man in Hollywood. It needs to be finessed."

"Bene," said Nico. "How do we communicate this?"

"A short statement to the press within the next twenty-four hours announcing the split. Reinforcing Evolution's historic commitment to women. I would say today, ideally, for the statement, but that may be unrealistic. Legal will want to go through it with a fine-toothed comb. Tomorrow morning, latest."

Nico nodded. "What about the ad campaign? We're going to need to pull it."

Giorgio, who looked remarkably unruffled, spoke up. "Online is no problem—we can cut it immediately. TV is the issue. It will take forty-eight hours to get the ad off the air."

During which time Evolution and Eddie would be inextricably linked in consumers' minds. Tension knotted Nico's stomach as he realized this wasn't going to be as simple as distancing the company from the actor with a quick statement. It was going to be far messier than that.

"Give me the names of the presidents of the networks if you have to," he bit out, fixing the older man with a stare. "I'll call them myself. I want that ad off the air, Giorgio. *Now.*"

"That will distance us from Eddie," Chloe broke in, "which we clearly want to do because the entire Vivre campaign is all about empowerment, and since three of our spokespeople are women, it's more about female empowerment than anything."

"Yes," said Cara. "Exactly. Soar might be in trouble, but we want to protect the other three fragrances and the investment we've made in them. The *brand.*"

A look of dismay crossed Chloe's face. Nico knew what she was thinking. Soar was her baby. Yet it was now synonymous with Eddie because she'd said publicly the actor had been the inspiration for it, a strategy that might cost her the fragrance.

He pushed on because sacrifices would have to be made. "What about Evolution's reputation when it comes to women?" he asked Cara. "How do we reinforce that?"

"We need to make a gesture of some sort. Underscore the commitment we've always had. But it can't be self-serving—it has to be genuine."

Nico raked a hand through his hair. "What about a philanthropic program for women? I'd been thinking we should build something off Vivre—use Lashaunta or Desdemona to kick it off."

"That's a great idea," Cara acknowledged, "if they aren't poised to drop us. It's a real possibility they could. Which is our next point of consideration," she said, eyeing Chloe and Mireille. "We need to get on the phone to them now. Reinforce everything we stand for. Make sure they don't jump ship."

They both nodded. "We can run the philanthropic idea past them while we do it," said Chloe.

Cara turned to Nico. "This would not be cheap.

We're talking millions. Are you prepared to invest in a program like this on a yearly basis?"

Nico looked grim. "We've staked the future of the company on Vivre. There's no turning back now."

Nico spent the day doing damage control with the PR team to prevent Evolution from being caught up in the public outcry that ensued over Eddie's vitriolic outburst about women that had been carried to every home in America via the amateur video it had been taken on.

Not only had the actor labeled his girlfriend, Camille, *a pointless piece of trash*, he'd dubbed women in general *an inferior species that are more trouble than they're worth*. Not to mention the punch he had allegedly thrown at his girlfriend, which, thankfully, in his drunken state, had missed.

With Evolution's public statement about the incident in legal review for distribution to the press first thing the next morning, Nico inhaled the key messages the PR team had developed for him in preparation for the press interviews that would come. But by early evening, a Boycott Evolution hashtag had appeared on Twitter, social media was ablaze with ironic amateur videos of Eddie's commercial spot edited to include his inflammatory comments about women and Nico was fighting the biggest crisis of his career.

By the time he made it back to the office after a dinner he'd been scheduled to attend, he was annihilated. Throwing his jacket over the back of a chair, he went to the bar to pour himself a drink. Froze with his fingers on the cap of the bottle of Scotch. Alcohol, thank goodness, had never been a problem for him like it had been for his father. But that had been before he'd drunk a good portion of a bottle of whiskey and given in to his craving for Chloe and put this disaster into motion. Because wasn't that exactly what had happened?

Pulling a bottle of spring water out of the fridge, he grimly poured himself a glass. He had *known* he should cut Eddie. But he had bet the bank on Chloe and her Vivre launch—on a suicidally risky campaign that would either revive the company or sink it, and he'd needed Eddie as the cornerstone of it.

The problem was, he wasn't impartial to Chloe.

Never had been. While he'd been making fifty-million-dollar decisions that affected the fate of the company, he'd been imagining what it would be like to bed her. Last night, when all hell had been breaking loose, he'd been buried *inside* her—putting the promises he'd made—Evolution itself—in jeopardy. Because his head hadn't been in the game, it had been on *her.*

He swore under his breath. Braced his palms on the bar. Clearly he *was* his father's son after all, because it was apparent he couldn't juggle his personal and professional life any better than his father had. Over what? Over a relationship he had a questionable ability to fulfill?

He'd seen the look in Chloe's eyes last night. She was in love with him. He had chosen to ignore it because as strongly as he felt about her, he wasn't *there.* He might never be there.

A cold knot tightened in his gut, the pressure that had been building in his head all day throbbing at his temples until he felt as if his head might explode. Had he not watched his father unravel himself over a woman, putting all he'd built into jeopardy? What the hell was he doing playing at something with Chloe he could never follow through on?

A part of him wanted to be that man. To be everything for her. But in reality, he knew how to do only one thing, and that was how to keep the boat afloat. To make this company prosper. And right now, he wasn't even doing a good job of that.

How the hell was he supposed to pull this out of the fire?

Chloe stood in the doorway of Nico's office, her stomach churning. It had been that way ever since she'd gotten the phone call from Mireille, but now it was worse because Nico had been freezing her out every time she'd been in the same room with him, and now she had to deliver more damaging news.

She took a deep breath and crossed to the window where he stood. He turned, as if sensing her presence, the look on his face as remote as it had ever been.

"I have an update on our celebrities."

He inclined his head for her to go on.

"Lashaunta," she said, "thankfully, seems unfazed. Which is a huge relief, because she can carry this for us. And she loves the philanthropy program. She's in, if it fits with her recording schedule.

"Desdemona," she continued, "worries me. She was very edgy on the phone, but when I explained the women's initiative to her, she said she'd consider it if we get the Eddie situation under control."

"That's positive."

"Yes." She bit her lip. Forced herself to deliver the bad news. "Estelle is out. Her agent wants nothing to do with it."

He looked remarkably calm. "If one jumps ship," he observed, "another could follow suit when they get wind of it. We need to work fast, ensure that doesn't happen."

"I told Lashaunta and Desdemona we'd get them details on the philanthropy program by the end of the week."

He nodded. "You and Cara can spearhead it together. Let me know what I need to know."

She inclined her head. "How was your dinner? Did you get any questions?"

"A few, but Cara had me prepped." His gaze

slid over her face. "Have you eaten anything today? You look pale."

"No—I'm not hungry." Needing his reassurance, his *comfort* right now, she lifted a hand to brush her fingers across his jaw. "I know you're angry with me and I understand why, but you can't freeze me out like this."

He caught her hand in his and brought it down to her side. "I'm not angry, Chloe. I'm focused. Go home, get some sleep. I'm going to stay here tonight and monitor things with the team."

Hurt lanced her insides, confusion enveloping her. "Nico, what's going on? Why do you look like that?"

That utterly inscrutable look remained painted across his face. "I don't think now is the right time for us to be having this discussion."

Her stomach turned to stone. "Why not?"

"Because we are in the middle of a *crisis*, Chloe. We need to be focused on fixing it."

That lit a fire inside her. "I *am* focused on fixing it," she bit out. "I've been killing myself all day to that end. We are going to fix this *together*, Nico, because your idea for the philanthropy program is brilliant. Because that's what a partner-

264 CHRISTMAS AT THE TYCOON'S COMMAND

ship is all about. But right *now*, I want to know what's going on with you. Why you're being like this."

"Don't push me," he said quietly. "You know better."

"Why not?" she demanded, ignoring the warning glint in his eyes, because her insecurities were ruling her now.

"Because instead of having my head on my shoulders," he bit out, "I've had it buried between your legs for weeks, that's why. Because I can't *think* when you are in my head, Chloe."

Her jaw dropped. "You cannot possibly be blaming this on us."

"No," he said evenly, "I'm saying it was a mistake. *We* are a mistake. I need to be focused on running this company."

She recoiled as if he'd struck her. "You're *ending* this?"

Not a flicker of emotion in those remote gray eyes. "I'm saying we need to cool it off."

Her heart contracted. He *was* ending it. He didn't have to say it. She could see it in his eyes. "Be honest, Nico."

He shrugged. "I told you from the beginning

what my capabilities are. We were both clear on what this is."

Her heart kicked against her ribs. She'd thought it had been *love*. She'd thought he had been falling in love with her. Had been so sure of it, she'd let down every last barrier for him so all he'd had to do was just admit it. Walk right into it. But seeing the impassive expression on his face, how easily he'd delivered that cutting blow, she realized he'd never really given them a chance. That she'd been the one who had been hopelessly deluded—at least when it came to his ability to evolve.

Because hadn't he done this to her *twice*? How many times did she need him to slap her in the face before she got it?

Except she knew where this was coming from. Knew his personal history was at play here. She knew *him* now.

"This is about your need for control," she said quietly. "You aren't in control of this situation. You aren't in control of *us*, so you'd rather choose to walk away than confront what we have. You'd rather use *this* as the perfect excuse to end it, when, in actual fact, we did exactly as you counseled, Nico. We made sound decisions. We listened to the experts, and they made the call. No one," she said, waving a hand at him, "could have predicted Eddie was going to go off the deep end. We all thought it was movie publicity."

"I did," he countered flatly. "And I should have listened to my instincts."

She had no response for that because he was right. He had.

He raked a hand through his hair. Eyed her. "It was always going to end with us, Chloe. It was just a matter of time. You know it and I know it. I am incapable of giving you what you need."

The way he so easily discarded what they had infuriated her. "I think you'd rather *believe* yourself incapable of love than expose yourself to it, Nico. Because then you'd have to allow yourself to *feel* something. Well, I'm not buying it for a minute. I've seen you with your brothers. I know your capabilities. They are miles deep. *Unconditional.* But they aren't on offer to me."

"They aren't on offer to anyone," he said evenly. "We have a good thing, Chloe. But what's going to happen when you want a man who can love you? Who can give you more? When you start to hate me because I can never give you that?"

It was a fair point. Because the way he was tearing her apart inside right now, she wondered if she was a bit on the masochistic side.

"I love you," she said quietly, before she closed herself off completely. "I have always loved you, Nico, you know that. You are the strongest, most admirable man I know. But if you walk away now, it's the last time, because you're right, not even I'm that much of a glutton for punishment."

His gray eyes glimmered with an emotion she couldn't read. "Better it happen now. Go home, Chloe. Get some sleep."

CHAPTER THIRTEEN

CHLOE WALKED HOME on a frozen Manhattan night, feeling as numb as the sheet of ice beneath her feet.

She shouldn't have pushed him like that. But if she hadn't, she never would have found out the truth. That, in his mind, Nico had never seen a future for them. That while she'd been spinning those romantic fantasies he'd warned her about, while she'd been offering him everything, he had been preserving those cast-iron walls he had perfected, never intending to let her in.

Letting herself in her front door, she shrugged off her coat and threw it on the bench in the hall. The cozy space felt unfamiliar, *foreign*, because she'd spent the better part of the past couple of weeks at Nico's place, caught up in the fantasy she'd spun for herself. It felt so empty it made her hurt inside.

She couldn't go curl up at Mireille's because

she was still at the office working with the team on the statement that would go out in the morning. Numb, utterly unsure of what to do with herself, she made some hot cocoa. Allowed herself a brief look at Twitter, which was a huge mistake. The Boycott Evolution hashtag had caught fire. There were thousands using it.

Her heart crawled into her throat, a feeling of dread twisting her insides. If they didn't contain this tomorrow, if their plan to announce the philanthropy program next week didn't turn the tide, Evolution and everything she'd worked so hard for would be in jeopardy. Everything her parents had entrusted to her.

She raked trembling fingers through her hair. It was all too easy to second-guess everything. Her overly ambitious launch plan, how closely she'd tied her fragrances to the personalities that represented them, how she'd ignored Nico's advice, when if she had listened, they wouldn't be in this situation.

It all ran through her head as she curled up and tried to fall asleep in her four-poster bed. *Alone.*

Hot tears stung her eyes, but there was also anger in that potent brew. Fury that Nico had been such a bastard to her. Fury that he would hide from himself like this, because she knew how he felt. Fury because she needed him now more than ever, his ability to right-side her world something she'd always depended on.

Blinking back the tears, she refused to cry. Refused to let *this* be the thing that felled her. She'd come too far for that. She'd become too much of a fighter. Nico was a *coward*, that was what he was. She would not be that.

She woke at an insanely early hour, just as dawn was creeping into the sky. A determination filled her, steely in its foundation. The massive sales, the overwhelmingly positive response to Vivre could not be wrong. She had not been wrong in her decisions. She could not abandon her vision now or it would all be for naught.

She might have been wrong about Eddie. She *had* been wrong about Eddie. So now she had to fix it. Unfortunately, she had a feeling this was going to get a lot worse before it got better.

It did get worse. By 9:00 a.m., Evolution's already fragile share price had dropped 20 percent and Nico was fielding calls from worried board members in between a seemingly endless number of press interviews, the media's thirst for Hollywood's latest scandal seemingly unquenchable.

Chloe took it upon herself to check in with her uncle to see if he'd made any progress on pulling the television ads before Nico flipped his lid. When Giorgio's PA announced he was on a call, she leaned against the doorway to his office and waited for him to finish. His back to her, his feet on the windowsill, she gathered it was Keith Taylor, one of the Evolution board members, on the other end of the line.

She frowned. Why was Giorgio talking to Keith? She didn't even think they knew each other. The gist of the conversation soon set her spine ramrod straight. *He was pressing his case with Keith as the man who should be running Evolution in the middle of a crisis that could bring the company down.*

Fury singed her blood. She was livid by the time Giorgio set the phone down and swung his chair around. His gaze sliding over Chloe, he had the audacity to wave her into a seat for a coffee with a lazy, self-satisfied expression on his face.

Chloe set her hands on her hips and raked a

look over her uncle, the resemblance to her father so strong it hurt sometimes. "You are *courting* the board in the middle of a crisis?" she breathed. "At Nico's expense?"

Her uncle shrugged. "It's the right time to get rid of him. You weren't so happy about him becoming CEO before you started sleeping with him."

She curled her hands into fists by her sides. He was out of control. Utterly out of line. How had she not seen it before? Had she been so deluded about *everything*?

"You're fired," she bit out. "Effective immediately."

Giorgio stared at her, astonished. "You can't do that."

"Father gave Nico the power to do it." She lifted her chin. "And I'm backing him up. This is unacceptable, Giorgio."

She marched out of his office. Absorbed the look of shock on his PA's face. "I will reassign you," she muttered, before she stalked into the hallway.

Her heart broken at her uncle's betrayal, she marched up to Nico's office, told her boss what

Giorgio had done and that she'd fired him, then burned a path to her own office, where she focused on the nascent philanthropy program she and the team were creating, keeping in touch with Lashaunta and Desdemona to update them on things and ensure they didn't jump ship. By the end of the week, she and the team had a platform they could brief the two stars on.

Lashaunta and Desdemona both loved the program, which would allocate millions over the next few years to women's causes, and both of them signed on. Helped in part by the fact that things on social media had gradually begun to calm down with Evolution's clear assurance the company had cut ties with Carello.

Lashaunta, with whom Chloe had developed a close relationship over the past few weeks, even agreed to fly to New York for the unveiling of the program, given she was already in America on tour.

By the time Chloe and Nico unveiled the program to hundreds of journalists at a press conference at Evolution, Lashaunta and Desdemona at their sides, Chloe was so exhausted she could barely put one foot in front of the other, investing everything she had left into the emotional remarks she made about why the program was so important to her—how everything she and her mother had ever done had been to empower women with their own particular kind of beauty.

When it was over, she knew she'd done everything she could. Now it was up to the world to decide Evolution's fate. What she could not seem to repair was her broken heart. It was still raw and bruised as Nico and she stepped off the podium and removed their mics.

"You were incredible up there," he said quietly, a warmth in his smoky gray eyes that had been missing for days.

She wrapped a layer of Teflon around her heart. Lifted her chin. "Because I knew we could do this together. Because we are a great team, Nico. That we can weather any storm together. It's you that didn't believe."

Nico stood looking out at a Christmas light extravaganza that was New York in December, nursing a Scotch as he surveyed the view from the floor-to-ceiling windows of his penthouse.

He thought Evolution might finally have turned

the corner today. Its stock price had rebounded after its disastrous drop and sales had done the same, with Be flying high again. The one price to pay from all of this might be Soar, of which sales had plummeted. But if that was the only casualty of this mess, he'd take it.

Ads for Be had been everywhere on his way home, plastered across the city, a big flashing reminder of the woman who had shown her steel spine today in that press conference with Lashaunta and Desdemona, passionately and fearlessly handling interviews with the major daily newspapers.

She was light-years from the woman he'd dragged home from Paris—a warrior. *Something to behold.* It cast his own inability to grow in far too harsh a light.

He'd spent the past couple of months forcing her out of her shell—insisting she evolve into what he knew she could be—even when it had meant stretching her to the very limits of her capabilities. Forcing her to acknowledge her innermost fears and expose them for the fraud they were. And what had he done? Reverted to old patterns—to a knee-jerk reaction to end things between them instead of taking a good look at himself. Instead of facing his own fears.

Chloe had been right. If he didn't allow himself to care about another person, if he didn't allow himself to *feel*, no one could destroy him like that ever again. Burying himself in his work, *providing* had been the only way he'd known how to survive. It was the way he'd operated since he was fifteen years old.

Which had been fine until Chloe had battered through his defenses with her courage and fire. Until she'd made him question his limitations. Made him want *more*. Until she'd made him want to *be* more. And that had scared the hell out of him.

He lifted the Scotch to his lips, welcoming its low, fiery burn. He missed her. He'd told himself his knee-jerk reaction to end them had been the right one, because dragging this affair out any longer was only going to hurt her more. Had buried himself in his work with twenty-hour days, expecting its usual anesthetic effects to function as it always did. But it hadn't.

Instead, her absence in his bed at night had only illuminated how lacking his life was in the spirit and warmth she brought to it. How being programmed as a machine to do only one thing wasn't enough anymore.

The problem was, he thought, staring out at a cavalcade of lights, he might have killed the one chance he'd had of having more because of a past that had owned him for far too long.

Christmas Eve had always been the most magical night of the year for Chloe. Right from the very beginning, when her father had read her and Mireille *The Night Before Christmas* in full theatrical voice while they sat on his lap at the house in Great Neck and drank big mugs of cocoa laced with her mother's candy cane syrup.

Later, when they'd gotten older, and Evolution had been founded, the magic had come from her father's big heart. He couldn't stand the idea of any of his employees spending Christmas alone, so he'd rounded them up like stray kittens and invited them to dinner, which had sometimes meant forty or fifty people at the table, her mother holding her head and muttering *numbers* the whole while.

But her mother had loved those boisterous, chaotic celebrations as much as Chloe and Mireille had. It was like the whole word had come to their big, warm, happy house on the hill.

And then there'd been the year the Di Fiore boys had shown up, looking shell-shocked in the middle of the crowd. Chloe thought she might have taken one look at Nico as he'd sat through her father's traditional end-of-year philosophical rant, so serious as he'd soaked it all up as if it was the most profound thing he'd ever heard, and fallen in love with him that instant.

But, she reminded herself as an ache surfaced deep inside her, she wasn't thinking about *him* right now. She and Mireille were going ice skating at Rockefeller Center, before they had wine and fondue at home. A new tradition. And she wasn't going to cry about that either, because Be was under half of Manhattan's Christmas trees, she knew her mother would be so proud of her and she was going to hold her memories close to her heart, exactly as Nico had said.

Damn him. He was everywhere.

Hat planted on her head, mittens at the ready, she tapped her foot impatiently on the hardwood floor. She had just glanced at her watch for the third time when a knock sounded on the door.

"You're late," she said impatiently, swinging the door wide. "Why is it I'm—" She stopped dead in her tracks at the sight of Nico standing on the doorstep, the memory of that kiss, that *show-stopping* kiss, flashing through her head.

Oh, no. She was not doing this tonight.

"Go away," she said firmly, refusing to acknowledge how beautiful he looked in jeans and a dark turtleneck sweater. "Mireille and I are going ice skating."

"Mireille isn't coming until later."

Her eyes widened. "Why not?"

"Because we need to talk." He gestured toward the door. "Can I come in?"

"No."

He sank his hands into her waist, picked her up and moved her aside. She gasped and gave him a furious look as he closed the door. "I don't want to talk to you. Nor do I want to kiss you until I lose my head. I want to go ice skating."

"Chloe," he said quietly, eyes on hers, "I need to talk to you. Hear me out and I promise I'll go away if that's what you want."

He looked serious, so serious she relented, toeing off her boots and leading the way into the living room. Perching herself on the sofa, she eyed him warily as he sat down beside her.

He raked a hand through his hair in an uncharacteristically fidgety move. "You were right," he began, "about why I pushed you away. This time and *every* time. Because I have always felt too much for you. Because you make me *feel* too much."

Her heart lodged in her mouth. "My father *was* a workaholic," he continued. "He was addicted to the buzz, but he was also addicted to keeping my mother happy. She messed with his head, she played him for all he was worth. If he'd *had* his head fully in the game, I'm not sure he would have made the mistakes he did, taken the risks he did, and maybe the outcome would have been very different."

She shook her head. "You can't say that. It may simply be that he had an addictive personality, a disease. To blame it on your mother is unfair."

His mouth compressed. "I'm not so sure. I went to see my mother, Chloe. That's how much you've turned my head upside down. I thought maybe you were right—that it would help me to understand better. Reframe things in my head."

Shock rendered her speechless. "What did she say?" she finally managed.

"That she was to blame for most of it. That she resented losing her career. She felt unequipped to be a mother, and she took it out on my father." He lifted a shoulder. "She also said she felt a great deal of sorrow about the decisions she's made."

"And did you believe her?"

"She seemed genuine about it." He rubbed a palm over the thick stubble on his jaw. "She said my father had the affairs to hurt her. To strike back. It became a vicious circle between them."

"Relationships are rarely simple," she murmured. "Even my parents, as in love as they were, had fights that would take down the rafters. They were passionate people. But the point is, they worked through it. They loved each other enough to make it work."

"Yes," he agreed. "They did." He dropped his head in his hands. Was silent for a moment. When he looked up, she saw the glitter of an emotion she couldn't read in his eyes. "I told myself I would never go on that kind of an emotional roller-coaster ride with a woman. I made *sure* I never did. But with you, I didn't have a choice. It just *was*. And when things fell apart with Eddie, it raised all my red flags and I mentally disengaged. A force of habit."

She shook her head. "We're better together, Nico. We are more *powerful* together. That's what held it all together. You and me."

"Yes," he acknowledged, "I know that now. But all of my baggage came into play. I started to question what I could be. Something Martino said to me." He rubbed a hand against his temple. "He saw us on the Fourth of July, Chloe."

Her jaw dropped, disbelief filtering through her. "He never said."

"He talked to me about it afterward. He told me to date you seriously or walk away."

She sank her teeth into her lip. "I can't believe he did that. It was *my* life."

"You were eighteen, Chloe. A baby. I was a hardened twenty-two. And he was right," he conceded. "I couldn't offer you what you needed. You needed to grow up and learn what life was all about. I already knew *too much* about life."

If she thought she'd been furious with her father

before, she was livid with him now. Because what would she and Nico have become if he hadn't interfered? What *could* they have become?

"So why are you here now?" she tossed at him, her insides hollow and empty, as if they'd been scraped out with something sharp. "If you're so sure you can never be what I'm looking for?"

His gaze locked with hers. "Because you've always been the best thing in my life. Because I was a fool to walk away from you again, and if you give me one more chance, I promise I won't mess it up."

"How do I know?" she whispered, hurt throbbing from the inside out. "I can't go through that again, Nico. Not one more time."

"Because I love you," he said, without missing a beat. As if they weren't the most earth-shattering words he'd ever uttered to her. "Because I've been in love with you a long time and I'm tired of fighting it."

Her heart skipped a beat. Hope bloomed inside her, so powerful, potent, it would have knocked her off her feet had she been standing. But there was also fear—fear he would do this to her again.

Clearly realizing how badly he'd screwed up, he

reached into his pocket and pulled out a brightly wrapped box. The blood in her veins pumped, jagged, erratic, as he sank down on one knee in front of her.

"Nico," she gasped, "what are you doing?"

"Proposing." He gave her an annoyed look. "I took Santo jewelry shopping, for God's sake. Let me get there."

Her stomach fell off a shelf and crashed to the floor. Oh, no, he wasn't doing this to her on Christmas Eve. The night fairy tales were made of.

"Marry me," he murmured, eyes on hers as he held up the most brilliant sparkling diamond she'd ever seen.

"Don't you think this is a bit extreme?" she breathed, eyes glued to the ring. "I forgive you. There, I've said it."

He shook his head. "It's always been you, Chloe. Always you."

That was it. She was done for. Forever and always.

She held out a trembling hand. Watched as he slid the brilliant diamond on her finger. It was like watching her most secret, most unobtainable fantasy come true. She couldn't speak, could only fling her arms around his neck as he gathered her up and sat down with her in his lap.

"I love you," she murmured against his amazing mouth. "So much. I've been so miserable, I think Mireille was dreading spending the evening with me."

"She's coming back. She's bringing Lazzero and Santo with her."

She pulled back. "You were that sure of me?"

He shook his head. "Willing to crash and burn."

Her heart contracted on a low pull. "I'll have one of those rather earth-shattering kisses now, thank you. You've earned it."

He gave her exactly that. When they finally came up for air, he pulled another box from his pocket. "One more."

She slid the box open to find a stunning Murano glass star nestled inside.

"So we can start our own traditions," he explained quietly. "Make new memories."

Her heart shattered. Turned to dust. But it was a good thing because with that last barrier smashed, she knew they would put each other back together again. Stronger. *Better.* Because that was what they'd always been about.

Nico stood with her in his arms. Boosted her up to set the star on top of the tree. She wrapped her arms around his neck as she stared up at it, glittering like the most gorgeous jewel in the sky.

"When did you say the others are coming back?"

He carried her toward the stairs. "*Later.* There's a tradition I'd like to start right now."

Her thoughts exactly.

* * * * *

LET'S TALK

Romance

For exclusive extracts, competitions
and special offers, find us online:

f facebook.com/millsandboon

⊙ @millsandboonuk

🐦 @millsandboon

Or get in touch on 0844 844 1351*

For all the latest titles coming soon,
visit millsandboon.co.uk/nextmonth